A Collection (

Short Stories

by

Darrel Hofland

CONTENTS

"A collection of peace where we could live
A collection of hope for us to give
A collection of words that mean we care
A collection of love for us to share"

Collective Soul

Dedication

To my brother, Warren
You have always encouraged me, fought for me, believed in me. Thank you.

To Lee,
I still can't get over how at least every month or two, you phone me, to see how I am doing. And this has been going on for years. Thank you.

Foreword

For the longest time, I have always wondered what I would write in a foreword. I know many years ago, in a previous foreword, I started with: Thank You Max Lucado.

And I will start there again. When I was 16, I discovered the books of Max Lucado. He introduced Jesus and the love of God and the Christian life in such an attainable and real way. He shared with ease how Jesus was in everyday things. Those earlier books I read made a profound impression on me. My love for reading and words probably started back then.

It's been a goal of mine for a very long time to have a physical book published. The time has now arrived! I am nervous and excited to share these stories with you. I have often pondered where ideas for people's stories come from. Some indeed have a brilliant imagination and I believe that others have written from their own life experiences. This is what I have done with these stories and pieces - I have captured various personal experiences and, in some ways, subtly included certain people in the pages.

I have always liked the idea that our lives include various chapters. There is a great Author and we live in the pages. And in each scene, we can be grateful for something. We choose to see wonder and delight in the big things as well as the small things of our stories. In the words of J.R.R. Tolkien:

"I wonder what sort of a tale we've fallen into?"

This is a collection of goods. Short stories, some *journal* entries and poetry. Maybe there is a line or a paragraph in the pages ahead that will encourage or inspire you.

Some of these words are over a decade old. Some of them may even be simple and perhaps, silly. But it's been a joy putting all of this together. I hope my words take you on a journey. I hope they make you smile. I hope they remind you that life is beautiful!

That Morning Sunrise

He paused as he noticed the graffiti on the wall.
WE LONG FOR CONECTION.

Andile smiled at the obvious mistake. Yet that truth tagged on the wall resonated within.

He pushed his board ahead of him and kickflipped off the pavement. Tomorrow he was going down to Durban with his skating sponsor, PEG Boards.

He loved the trendy artistic feel to Newtown in Johannesburg, but there was something about that beachfront in Durban that he longed for, he felt connected there.

However, before his trip, he would use the first few hours of the morning mastering his skill. The curbs, stairs and rails scattered around this transformed inner city made for an excellent training ground. It was in Newtown that he was spotted by a local skate store owner, who asked to film his skills. That YouTube clip circulated quickly and lead to many open doors for Andile, plus sponsorship and training.

After her cappuccino, Angie got up, left the money under the sugar jar and headed north along the promenade, her camera slung over her shoulder. This was her favourite time of the day. The natural light created a beautiful ambience around the beachfront.

She was looking forward to capturing another great shot of the setting sun behind the Moses Mabhida Stadium. The massive arch that extends over the pitch looks incredible against the backdrop of the sky filtered by the sinking sun. When she pushed that button and snapped away, Angie was

1

at peace. She forgot about the voices inside demanding her attention.

He wondered what his name was. This question had racked his brain a few times a day and had been the case for over the past year. He didn't ask anymore how he had got here. That question was irrelevant now. The smell he carried was more comforting than the shame he wore. A few years back she had kicked him out. He never saw that coming. She was his everything. She was his sunshine. (as he once sang in a homegrown song, he had written for her.) Now that was a long-gone memory - certainly, in *her* mind.

I wonder what my name is.

She had said, 'your life is going to amount to nothing if you keep up at this rate. It is never ever one bottle with you. You're drinking our money away!' He had heard her threats but didn't pay attention to them. Then it was too late! And now look at him. He was scraping together the coins that tourists and locals had tossed at him. His staple diet was a loaf of bread each day. And the occasional stick of glue.

What is my name?

May sat on her stoep as the evening sky pushed the daylight away. She loved her early evening cup of tea and reading session. Mrs. May Weatherly had written a fair number of short stories in her earlier years. Now, after many decades having rolled on, she still was still in love with stories but didn't write anymore. Instead, each week she ploughed through at least four books.

These stories and places kept her mind sharp and active. The many characters from those pages had been constant friends. Oh how she still missed her late husband after eight years. Around his and her birthdays and their anniversary she would set an extra place at the table. No, that little ritual didn't help with the healing and moving on. But she questioned why people were so obsessed with always trying to erase memories.

Mr. Weatherly had been an outdoors man. He had a huge love for wildlife, especially identifying birds. He had a keen eye and could spot and correctly name a great number of species.

When he was alive, at least twice a week they would make their way down to the beach to watch the sunset. It was "their little date time" and after he had passed on, May still made the effort to go down every so often to Durban beachfront. The hive of activity and hordes of people seemingly *floating* by, made her feel safe and connected. She remembered how her husband would comment on the sensation of the soft sand sifting through their aging toes. She grinned once again at the thought.

Andile landed around 3pm in Durban. The flight had been a bit too turbulent for his liking and he was thrilled to be on solid ground again. He wasn't a fan of that sort of flying. However, the *air* he got on some of his tricks; now that was *flying* that really exhilarated him! He waited at the 'pick up and go' area wearing his sponsored tee shirt, board bag and backpack. His driver, Moses, was always on time. Moses and Andile exchanged greetings and Andile asked if there would be time to head to the beachfront before they arrived at the hotel. Moses nodded.

The filming for the advert was set to start the next day. Andile was hoping he would catch the sunset, a sight and time of the day he always loved about those Durban trips.

Angie's following with her WordPress blog and Instagram account had grown rapidly over the last year. Her expression of photography and poetry had gained a keen audience very quickly.

She, like others, found solace with online community. Getting many 'likes' and comments always made her feel appreciated. It seemed the words and pictures that she married together resonated with her 'followers'. But still that emptiness hung over her, like wearing a rain-soaked coat. She was approaching thirty and no man had noticed her - the guys she had met with before just wanted to score. *Where were all the gentlemen?* She longed to be cherished. To be appreciated for her skills and her personality. But her life seemed like she was in a waiting room. Waiting. For way too long. But to no avail. She longed for more than just an online connection.

The elderly couple walked past and threw some coins at him. He sat parched on the pavement. He counted their *pathetic* offering. R3.50; what was that going to get him?

He heard the man complain to his wife: "Bloody beggars ruining the atmosphere on the beach." He longed to recall his name. He was more than just these ragged clothes that he wore.

What is my name? I wish someone would take time to get to know me. I am surely not all that bad.

The night was approaching quickly. He would need to head for the piers to find his shelter. He hid his only blanket there. At least under the piers he had some protection from the chilly nights. *Tomorrow would be a new day.* Repeating that, kept him going.

The day had escaped her. May had missed her scheduled visit to the beachfront. She had blamed the latest story she had lost herself in - *Blue Horizon* by the famous Wilbur Smith. She would have to go the following morning and watch the sunrise. It was only early autumn, so it wouldn't be too cold for her.

After meeting up with his tour manager, Andile was given a filming schedule for the next day and he was given the rest of the evening off. He decided to flick across the channels and he saw that Chelsea was playing Manchester United - a good game to watch. So, he sat back on the sofa and lost himself in the game.

He then browsed through the schedule for the next day. His filming only started at 9am. Perfect! He could go and watch the sunrise for a change. That prospect excited him.

After going through the photos of the stadium, Angie marvelled at her new creative shots.

Tomorrow I should go take some sunrise pictures of the Indian Ocean.

Maybe an early morning visit to the beach would be restoring for her soul.

21h00.

Those four people from vastly different backgrounds didn't realize that the new day would bring something new and beautiful for each of them.

Andile, a sponsored skater.

Angie, a talented but lonely photographer.

The beggar who had forgotten his name.

May Weatherly, a widow who loves words.

Lost in their dreams. Those four lives sound asleep.

It was as if a beautiful serenity hung over the city of Durban.

If one could step outside of the atmosphere and look down upon the earth, they would understand how a night like this looked and felt. Oh, starry night. All is calm.

May was awoken by the chirping of the birds in her garden.

The hotel lobbyist called Andile at 5am to wake him up - he was going to take a run down to the beach.

He, (who did not know his name) heard the street cleaners walking up and down the promenade and guessed it was rather early. About 05h30 in the morning.

Angie's phone alarm set for 05h30 had started to sing to her. She had set the song: "Where the Streets have no Name" by U2 as her alarm tone. Bono's soothing voice always inspired her! *How does one ever get bored of U2?*

Soon the sun would peer over the horizon, bringing some strangers together.

The weather forecast said that the sun would rise at 06h17. May parked her car at the North Beach parking lot. So did Angie who arrived about twenty minutes later.

Andile got there about 06h00. He had run about 2km from the hotel to North beach. *What a great start to the day*!

After catching his breath, Andile walked towards the sea. He gazed to his left. Under the pier he saw a man shuffling around and getting up. A wave of compassion swept over him. He thought he should at least get him a coffee and greet him. He glanced backwards and noted the corner café on the promenade was already open. *Typical foreign businessman; always wanting to make the extra buck!*

However, this time Andile was grateful. He went in and bought two coffees. As May headed towards the beach, she noted the young lady also walking towards the sea. They both seemed to place their feet on the sand at the same time.

She had a camera hanging from her neck.

Angie glanced to her right noticing the old lady also at the beach at this time. The beach seemed rather busy this morning. Clearly watching the sunrise seemed like the order of the day! They stood about fifteen metres apart. Angie looked at her watch. Six minutes to go. May decided that she would stand closer to the young lady.

"It's a beautiful morning!" she said out loud.

Angie turned and smiled, "Most definitely! A wonderful way to start a day."

They introduced themselves and the conversation after that flowed so easily. Andile approached the pier with the two cups in his hand. The *nameless* man looked up and saw this young man approaching him. He tried to neaten himself up, a seemingly impossible task wearing dirty creased clothes. He at least had his fingers to comb his hair a bit. As Andile approached the beggar, he paused, and memory caught up with him.

Wait a minute!

"Joe, is that you?"

The beggar squinted his eyes to observe this young guy who seemed to have recognized him.

"Joe Reece is that you?"

Tears streamed down his face. *That's who he was!*

Andile helped Joe remember that a few years back he was his guitar teacher.

"You were so good at guitar!" Andile said.

Joe stepped forward and hugged him. In that moment he felt connected! Andile had given Joe back his dignity. Joe explained his recent name dilemma as they watched the sunrise together sipping on their coffee. A little further along the beach as the sun greeted the new day, May hinted to Angie: "You would love my grandson. He is artistic too!" Angie smiled at that thought.

That morning connections were made. Life is full of surprises!

(Written: 31 March 2014)

Grandpère's words

Lauren sat there before the dawn broke. She held the cup of coffee close to her cheek - the warmth was comforting. It was those little moments that added to her life. It was her mom who taught her to appreciate the small things in life. *They were the little pieces of a glorious jigsaw puzzle!*

But on that morning, her spirit was disturbed - it was her son, Jack - he had lost his joy. She was losing grip of her son and she just didn't know how to reach him. He was in a slump and she wanted to get him out. Jack himself would admit that he too was losing grip of his own life. He spent hours in his room sometimes only coming down for meals and would eat in silence or with only one-worded answers:

"How was school day?" she would ask.

"Fine"

"Are you enjoying the omelette? Ham and cheese is your favourite."

"Yes"

Then they would fall back into silence. She hated seeing her son like this. He never went outside anymore. His screen time was escalating! She sat there trying to imagine his world - at fifteen he had the weight of the world on his shoulders. *But was all that weight necessary?*

Jack would hover from one profile to another on Instagram – seeing how "amazing" people's lives were. He was comparing them with his own life, wondering why his own selfies would not get as many likes as his classmates. *What's wrong with me?* The social pressure to be popular was swallowing him whole - he was drowning!

The key rattled in the lock and they could hear the door swing open - Paul was home.

He came into the kitchen - full of life and even after six hours of travel, he was beaming!

"They accepted my proposal!" he announced.

"That's wonderful, honey." Lauren replied, half-heartedly. Jack just stared at his plate.

Paul could feel the despondency of the room, but he refused to succumb to it. Lauren gave him that look – and right then, he knew what had to be done.

"Right! In an hour, we're heading off to see Grandpère - road trip! Each of you, go pack your bags!" he declared.

Jack looked up. "It's Thursday, what about school?"

"I'm sure you won't mind missing two days," Paul replied, winking at his son. "Now, go pack."

Lauren smiled at her husband - he was full of good ideas - *what is his plan this time?*

As if he could read her thoughts, he told her how he believed a trip to the countryside would help and that his dad would know what to do with their son. She got up and hugged Paul.

"You must be exhausted!"

"I am, but this is important." He smiled at her, then dialled his dad's number:

"Comment vas tu?" he asked.

"Bien merci," his dad replied.

He went on to explain the purpose of their visit. Jack's Grandpère was excited to see them - it had been six weeks since their previous visit.

With their bags packed, they buckled up and were ready to head off. Paul prayed for travelling mercies. Lauren squeezed his hand - they were desperate for a miracle. Jack held his phone tightly. *That thing would be the death of him if he kept using it as a source of validation.*

10

After an hour of driving, Paul had an idea: they would pull over at the next picnic stop. (He had done that different route once or twice before, so had an idea of what the next stop was like.) As he turned off, he could see the enquiring look from Lauren.

"Let's take a family photo." he suggested. "Please can we use your phone for that?" Paul asked Jack.

What is Paul up to? He's encouraging our son to use his phone.

"Where are we, anyway?" Jack asked, trying to add some nonchalance to his question. Paul smiled at his son - he was glad that he had noticed the change of route.

"Good observation! We're not going to Grandpère's!"

Jack and his mom looked at Paul quizzically and before they could ask questions, he continued: "We are seeing Grandpère, but he and I decided on another venue for the weekend. We're going to Fantasy Lodge."

"Where's that?" Jack's mom asked.

"Wait and see! Now, let's do this photo."

They had pulled over at one of those 'half-moon' concrete-slabbed stops. There was a knee-high wall that wrapped around the circumference of that open space which was made of concrete and medium sized rocks – about half a metre in height. Over to the left were two concrete picnic tables and on the right, there was another.

That stop was significant for me although my dad (and even I) didn't realise it at the time. But my rescue began there, looking into the gorge...

As Paul and Lauren stood ready for the photo, Paul noticed how his son sprang up on the wall and peered into the gorge. He was drinking in the view as if were a full glass of fresh orange juice – savouring each sip. To the right of where they had stopped, the gorge went upwards, filled in by lush green trees. A forest so thick that the sunshine battled to break through. To the left, it opened with a river running down into the open landscape below. Across the gorge on the east side, there was a bush halfway up, covered in ruby-red foliage, above which an inviting silence seemed to hover. In the distance, one could faintly hear the water running below. *A non-disturbing noise.*

"Ready? Cheese!" Jack asked as he positioned himself just in front of his parents.

After three or four photos, Jack considered the valley one last time.

"Okay, all aboard," Paul shouted as he headed back towards the car. "We have about an hour to go."

After driving through some old mountain passes with vast fields to the left and right, the mood in the vehicle seemed lighter.

Grandpère was sitting on the porch when they arrived. He was engrossed in a novel.

"You've made yourself at home, I see."

"This is not the place," he winked, "this is the reception." Paul greeted his dad the customary French way: a kiss on each cheek. Grandpère instructed them to leave the vehicle to the right of the building, take their things and jump in the old-school 4x4 Ford Cortina bakkie that he had parked on the left.

"We're going about two kilometres down the road… Hello Jack, good to see you. Ça va?"

Jack didn't look up. "Fine, thanks." (Lauren smiled. *A two worded answer this time.*)

"Come greet me properly, please." After the two kisses, Grandpère pulled in Jack and gave him a bear hug.

"Aagh! Grandpère!"

Grandpère just chuckled and playfully punched his grandson on the shoulder *as guys do.*

Two kilometres down the dirt road they had arrived. With his arms raised up as if he were making a loud declaration, Grandpère, beaming, spoke:

"Welcome to Fantasy Lodge. You're going to have a fantasy.... *fantastic...* Fantasy Lodge... *see what I did there?*"

They all smiled. His enthusiasm was contagious and appealing and they totally understood why when they saw where their accommodation:

"Wow, this is amazing!!" It was Jack who spoke first.

Standing before them, was a three-storey tree house, on stilts. Behind it was a sea of trees - part of an immense lush forest. For as far as the eye could see, they were surrounded by these welcoming green giants, with the occasional tree house sprouting up between them.

"There are ten tree houses, altogether," Paul said, "I read that on their site."

"Shotgun the top floor." Jack exclaimed. He even helped with his mom and Grandpère's bags.

Lauren smiled at this obvious change in her son.

The treehouse was fully stocked - it was brilliant! From bedrooms on each floor to a living room, to a jacuzzi, the viewing deck on the roof, the furniture and other décor were all so delicately carved from wood. So masterfully well done!

That afternoon, Grandpère took them for a looped walk around the forest. He was acting like a big kid, and they couldn't help but follow his lead - at one point, Grandpère, with the help of Lauren, insisted that Paul and Jack should be covered in leaves.

That afternoon they hugged trees and threw pine cones. It was like they were living in a fantasy - but it was all so real and all so wonderful!

Near their treehouse, Grandpère pointed to a spot: four trees had made a natural square. Each tree stood on the corner as if they were the posts of a boxing ring. Grandpère, full or random but fun ideas, pointed at the first tree: "Jack, you sit there."

Then he pointed at the next tree, "Paul, you are over there." And then he turned to Lauren: "the third tree there."

He pulled out those popular small glass Coke bottles: "Cheers!"

There they sat, legs stretched out in front of them, no words exchanged - just them soaking in the moment. Paul could see contentment in his son's demeanour.

That night, Lauren sat snug in bed reading her book while the guys were huddled around the fireplace.

"Jack, grab your sleeping bag and a pillow. I want to take you're right to the top, if that's okay?" Grandpère invited.

Jack beamed back. "Cool!"

Paul knew his dad and son needed that time together and he wasn't quite tired yet - so he continued stoking the fire and watching the flames whilst sipping on a glass of Merlot.

They climbed the stairs next to Jack's room on the top floor. From there a ladder led up to the rooftop of the treehouse. Grandpère and Jack climbed through a trapdoor onto the roof above. The cool air of the autumn night greeted them - it was a little chilly. Then Jack looked up and gasped! The sky was filled with thousands and thousands of stars, no city lights tainting the natural night-time sky. It was like a black canvas with pin pricks in it – and a golden yellow light piercing through.

They climbed into their sleeping bags and just lay there, Grandpère and Jack, side by side. For about half-an-hour they gazed upwards, in silence, nature obliged and sent three or four shooting stars overhead. In the corner of his eye, Grandpère could see his grandson smiling.

"He put a new song in my mouth, a hymn of praise to our God." Grandpère quoted a Psalm from the ancient scriptures. Jack thought about that. Seeing all these shimmering and shooting stars, one couldn't help but respond in awe and gratitude! *Such spectacular beauty deserved a song of praise - to say the least!*

After another half hour of silence, Grandpère spoke again: "In a world full of stories, you can only live out yours." With those words, Jack felt something inside of him - like his heart was jumping up and down in agreement with that statement. *"Yes, yes!"* it seemed to say.

Grandpère then sat up, squeezed his grandson's hand, smiled at Jack and Jack smiled in return. Grandpère got up and headed back towards the trapdoor - as he placed his feet on the first rung of the ladder, he looked across to Jack lying there:

"No one is better than you."

And then Grandpère disappeared through the trapdoor. Jack was left alone up there with those six words and the stars and a change of heart. There was nothing arrogant about that statement. The words just seemed to gently fall into Jack's spirit. He felt happy! He felt alive! And somehow, he knew those were not just fleeting feelings.

Jack wrestled with his thoughts: the long drive, Grandpère's words, the lessons of nature he learnt during the trip, his lack of self-belief, his wasted energy on trying to be like one of the cool kids. *Did getting many likes on social media really matter?*

He knew he had to spend less time on his phone - it was *killing* him. And just a waste of time! He knew too that *comparison was the thief of joy*. And out there on the roof top, he heard the unspoken invite of the stars:

"Go live! There is a lot more to explore."

Jack felt blissful! The stars shimmered with excitement. Jack's eyes grew heavy as the tiredness from the full day finally caught up with him. He fell asleep.

In about five hours, a new day would dawn. And a *new* boy would arise.

The Unexpected Playlist

Playlist
/ˈpleɪ|ɪst/

noun

a list of songs selected with thought to be played by another.

verb

NB. one does not just randomly put a playlist together. There needs to be purpose in the selection of songs.

1 (Seth)

He sat there on the edge of his bed, thinking. At twenty-five, he wanted to be somewhere else. Dressed in his green Quiksilver hoodie and a pair of boardshorts, Seth felt there was a world "out there" calling him to new horizons.

For the past four years, in a little coastal town in South Africa, he had worked in the local music store. But he was no ordinary employee. Music was his passion. He knew his stuff. Customers enjoyed being served by Seth. The way he spoke of music and lyrics and that glimmer he would get in his eyes, showed his keen interest in music. He was often frustrated by his fellow colleagues who knew *diddly-squat* about music. It was like they were just working there to pass time or make a quick buck.

"Music is powerful. It can transport you." Seth convincingly said to himself. Seth felt in his bones that somehow music would take him places. How could knowing so many lyrics, facts about bands and the constant popping up with the perfect lyric not amount to something?

Now a strange thing had happened earlier that day during his morning shift. As he said that mantra of his: "music is powerf…," a customer in the neighbouring aisle finished his sentence: "…ful. It can transport you." He had this smirk on his face and then headed for the exit. Seth scrutinized him. The mystery man spoke again: "I've got something for you. See you soon." And then he turned and headed out into the car park, disappearing in the bright glare outside.

Now a few hours later in his room, he thought of that incident with the mystery man. He had never seen him in the store before, and being observant, he had a general idea of who came in and out.

"Supper's ready!" He heard his mother call from the kitchen. Leaving his thoughts in the room, he headed downstairs to dine with his mom. Dinner was a delicious stir fry. Before heading off to bed, Seth opened his bedroom window and let the cool breeze drift in. He gazed at the stars.

His life was often filled with music, so that little evening ritual of silence was something he treasured and did his best to keep. That silence soothed his soul.

2

Later that week, during his afternoon shift that "mystery man" came into the store holding a box. He headed towards Seth.

"Here is what I promised you. Enjoy it. The songs will show you things. Use it wisely. And please don't forget to charge it!" He paused. "Otherwise you may be stuck somewhere else."

He paused again. "Then again, you may want that."

"Um, thanks!" replied Seth, hesitantly. The man gave a warm smile.

"Hey mystery man, do I know you? What's your name?" Seth asked holding his fingers as inverted commas when he said: "mystery man."

"Does it matter? Even the streets have no names." The man in turn held his fingers up in inverted commas.

"Touché" Seth replied. *Did he just quote U2 to me?*

The man continued, "But I like that, call me: mystery man, if naming me is important." He paused. It looked as if he was thinking of the right words to use. "Sometimes our prayers are answered, right?" He chuckled, reached for Seth's shoulder, patted him, then turned for the exit.

"Godspeed Seth…"

Wait, how does he know my name?

As if reading his thoughts, the man spoke again: "Don't forget your name badge."

Seth took the gift to the back room of the store. It was a quiet morning - no customers had ambled in yet. He unwrapped the parcel to find an iPod Nano. Seth felt appreciative that he had a sort of relic in his hands. However, he also thought that the present seemed a little redundant. He worked in a music store, surrounded by songs, so this device seemed a little pointless or clichéd. The store doorbell rang so Seth left the gift in his locker and went to serve the customer. The day seemed to move slowly with Seth's mind wondering what songs the man had put on the iPod. *What did he mean by: the songs will show you things?* He hadn't looked yet because he was one of those people who, when getting a new album, would sit on his bed with the CD sleeve, going through the lyrics while the entire disc played. He always wanted to learn the lyrics and try to decipher what the songs were about.

5pm.

He unlocked his bicycle and pedalled out of the car park towards the main road. Seth often cycled without his iPod, but when he did, he would always have only one earpiece in. That way, he would have a soundtrack to his cycling but could also hear the city and the rushing wind whizzing past him.

Four km. twelve minutes. It usually took him about that time to get to and from home. Seth's day seemed to have a few rituals that he really liked to keep. Riding his bike was one of them. He liked how life looked from his pedals. He often noticed how people seemed so shut off in their cars, their windows up, seeming detached from the people walking the streets.

From his bicycle, he could hear the locals speaking to their friends, shouting orders or even just whistling to themselves. The hustle and bustle of the pedestrians, as he skilfully manoeuvred through them, gave Seth a sense of connection to life outside his sphere.

After supper that night, Seth had some alone time. He and that mysterious gift of an iPod. What songs would be on there? He sat on his bed, wearing his favourite hoodie and boardshorts again. Underneath he still had his work shirt on, and he hadn't taken off his Converse shoes either. It seemed the excitement of the gift altered his routine. He turned on the iPod and glanced at the song list. He saw there were between fifteen and twenty songs on it. Seth felt a surge of disappointment. Probably about two thirds of the songs he already knew. *I was rather overly excited just for this.*

He read to himself some of the artists that were on there. *Linkin Park, Funeral for a Friend, Straatligkinders and Relient K.*

20

He plugged in his earphones. He did not realise his life was about to drastically change.

3

Seth decided to select a track by Straatligkinders called "Die avontuur van n' hartbreek" (*translated: the adventure of a heartbreak*). He chose it because of the intriguing song title. Clicked PLAY.

FLASH!!!

It all happened so fast. Everything around Seth seemed to close in on him as a bright and almost blinding light filled his vision and then he heard a very loud swirling noise. It would have probably deafened him; however, the earpieces muffled the sound. Then, there seemed to be a minute or so that lapsed from his recollection.

PITCH DARK.
THEN LIGHT REPLACED THE DARKNESS.

He slowly opened his eyes, the song he had selected still playing. Seth noticed how suddenly cold he felt. He could not believe what he was seeing and where he was. In utter shock and confusion, he just sat down to try and grasp what had just happened.

He immediately jumped up with a cold bum because the ground was blanketed in snow. In fact, he wasn't even on level ground. He was high up a mountain. Surrounding him, he noticed incredible peaks also steeped in snow. It was then that he started taking in everything else. There were plenty of people around him, all dressed in ski gear, either with skis attached to their feet or a snowboard under their arms. A sense of delight was in the air. He then read a nearby sign: Morzine, France. A wooden cabin was behind with a first aid logo stuck upon the door. He headed towards it to escape the cold. A group of teenagers pointed and laughed at him, noticing that he was only wearing boardshorts and a hoodie.

What was going on? Seth was desperate for an explanation.

The song played on in his earpieces, but he needed silence. He needed to work out what was going on. He reached for the iPod and pressed PAUSE.

FLASH!!!
BLINDING LIGHT. WHISSHH!!
PITCH DARK.
LIGHT REPLACING THE DARKNESS.

Again, he opened his eyes. Seth was back, sitting on his bed, his legs suddenly warm again. *Could this really be?*

His mantra popped into his mind: "Music is powerful, it can transport you."

Did that song just send me to some place in France?

He was tempted to press play again. He looked down at his iPod. There was a little piece of paper sticking out from behind the iPod under its cover. He pulled it out and read:

Once you a select a song, you cannot skip to the next one until the song has played its full duration.

So, enjoy each moment.

MM.

Seth smiled to himself. *Nice touch! MM for Mystery Man.* What was happening to him wasn't logical or even possible, but it wasn't the time to try and work out the science or the possibility of the phenomenon that rested in the palm of his hand. He wanted an adventure. And it was

22

right there with him, luring him in. No time to waste. He jumped off his bed, grabbed his backpack from the cupboard and thought of what he should bring with him. He always tried to live according to the scout motto that he had learnt a few years ago:
BE PREPARED.

4

He put on some jeans and found a beanie to wear. He also packed a backpack full of items he deemed necessary for his adventure: a scarf, boardshorts, socks, underwear, a spare shirt, some gloves and his passport too. He then added his wallet, a torch, pen, notebook, his camera and a charger. It was exciting trying to put just enough and not too much all into one bag. There was a slab of chocolate and pack of biscuits that lay in a plastic bag on his desk. He grabbed that too.

He decided then that he was ready, put the backpack on and sat on his bed again. He reached down to press PLAY. The same process as before, probably about 45 seconds altogether.

FLASH.
BRIGHT LIGHT. WHISSHH!!
PITCH DARK.
RECOVERING LIGHT.

There was about 2 minutes 44 seconds left of the song. Seth heard the crunching of snow below. He headed back for the guard hut he had seen earlier. This time the cold was not as biting on his legs. A man opened the door looked him over and greeted him in French.

Darn it, I should have packed a French phrase book.

23

"Bonjour," Seth replied.

A broken conversation of French and English followed. Seth managed to arrange a pair of snowboarding boots and a board. He had just shy of 2 minutes left. He hoped he would be a quick student - thankfully, he was!

That crisp air up on those mountains rushed past his cheek. He felt alive as he saw the ground racing below him. He glanced at the time left. 15 seconds. A tinge of sadness filled him. Then, he just tried his luck. *What the hell; let me just try this.* He pressed the reverse skip button. The song restarted. And he was still on the slope. He smiled and then panicked. He didn't notice the turn ahead. Up off the *piste* he went into a mound of snow.

Phssh!!! A flurry of snow and Seth were both hurled into the air. Thankfully, the landing was soft. He chuckled to himself. *This is really happening! I am surrounded by snowy mountains, snowboarding!!*

"Woohoo!" he shouted. There was a minute and 36 seconds left of the song, so he tightened his boot holds, got up and carried on down the slope. He was singing along to his iPod. Adventure had caught up with him. He was now at the bottom of the slope and laughed at the inevitable, he wasn't going to be able to stop gracefully! *Oh well.* He veered a little away from the clusters of people and tried a little jump as he reached the end. Smash! He ploughed into a mound of old snow. Sniggering, he got up and dusted off the snow, then unstrapped the remaining foot from the board. He reached his arm behind to see if his backpack was secure. He looked down at his iPod and didn't press PAUSE. 7 seconds left. *What next?*

5

Same procedure:

FLASH.
BRIGHT LIGHT. WHISSHH!!
PITCH DARK.
RECOVERING LIGHT.

The next song was by Linkin Park: Shadow of the Day. Seth found himself walking on a pavement. The sun that met his skin was warmer and the bite in the air had vanished, but there was still a freshness about his surroundings. *Where am I?*

He saw a street sign stating the road he was on: Folly Lane. He noticed how narrow the road was, so "lane" was an apt description. He heard the chatter of kids at play in a nearby park. He looked up at the clear blue sky and heard his shoes scratching along the pavement under his steps. Wherever he was, he could tell that summer was being awakened. There were blossoms peering out at him and the leaves on most trees looked a giddy green. Seth walked on for another five-hundred metres, just soaking in the experience. He finally came across some more people that seemed to be gathered in a town centre of some sorts. It was clearly market day. A whole array of stores stood before him, stall owners shouting out their specials. He heard a couple nearby speak softly to each other. On hearing their accents, he realised that he was in England. Then he saw signs stating the distance to surrounding towns. The song he was listening to was about to end. He re-started it…

Seth felt peckish. He spotted a take-away called Subway. His stomach grumbled. Those subs displayed on the posters looked delicious. He went in and ordered one with meatballs and cheese.

In a strong accent, the man behind the counter said: "Three pounds fifty, please."

Seth unconsciously pulled out a five-pound note. *Hang on. How did I get pounds in my wallet?*

He didn't care. He smiled at his good fortune and reaching for his iPod, he started the song again.

I wonder how many times I can restart a song on this iPod.

For the duration of the song, he sat at a table on the sidewalk looking at the hive of activity from the market. He then saw the name of the city in the middle of the market square: St Albans.

40 seconds left of the song…

6

The iPod selected a song by Taking Back Sunday: Summer, Man. Seth found himself looking down a speedometer reading seventy miles per hour, driving in what seemed to be some family car. It was spacious and it was cruising. He noted the racing countryside slipping by. His windows were wound down a fraction and the cool morning air was climbing in. He saw on the passenger seat next to him there was a bible and what seemed to be some notes for a talk. *Perhaps a sermon?*

He smiled to himself. *What situation had this song taken him to?* He saw a sign ahead saying Silverstone: sixteen.

He had heard about Silverstone on TV; it was a famous Formula 1 racetrack - and there he was heading towards that village. He saw too that there were printed directions on the seat beside him. He grabbed them and worked out whereabouts on the route he was. Once he got his bearings, he peered out the windows and absorbed his surroundings. He was still in England but in another part. Ten miles to go.

He restarted the song and counted the colours around him. There was white from the wispy clouds that hung above. There was the light blue of the morning sky. The fields of rapeseed flowers sported the colour yellow. The trees waving as the car whizzed past wore green foliage and of course, the orange glow of the sunrise was fading as the day awoke.

Five miles left. He decided to pull over in the next layby, then picked up the talk notes to see what the topic was. Panic enveloped him. *I can't do this!* He wondered what would happen when he arrived at his destination - surely the people there wouldn't know who he was. Seth arrived there a little before 10am. 14 seconds left of the song. He was tempted to let the song end and just leave the scene, but this was part of the adventure, he didn't want to cower out of it.

He reached down and gasped!! The iPod had just powered off. The silence in his earpieces met the noisy chatter of people outside welcoming others to their little church in Silverstone. Seth sat there for what seemed like a long time, wondering what was going to happen. With the iPod switched off, did that mean he was stuck there?

He then noticed someone coming towards him. So, he smiled and decided to just roll with it. Leaving the safety of the car, he stepped out onto the pavement.

"Hi, Seth, good to meet you. We've heard that you're replacing our regular preacher who has been taken ill." Seth swallowed and smiled. *How did they know his name?*

"Um, hi, thank you. It's good to be here."

"I'm Eric. Let's go and grab something to eat."

On the way in he noticed the old stonework of the church building and sensed that there was a lot of history engraved in the walls.

27

Once he stepped inside, he was greeted by warm smiles, some hellos and the delicious smell of freshly cooked bacon and eggs. *Wow, a cooked breakfast at church!*

His mind briefly drifted from the present to inside his head. *I wonder how I am going to leave this "scene" that I am in?* Just then, he was snapped back to reality by a toned-down argument behind him. He heard a mother talking to her teenage son: "Can you not just be present for one moment in your life, and not wish it away?" The boy took out his earpieces and mumbled his reply: "okay." It felt like Seth was meant to hear that argument. He too felt challenged - to be more present and not worry about "the next step." So, he let of his concern.

He headed toward the coffee table and chatted with a gentleman there who was adding two sugars to his cup. After some small talk and almost finishing his coffee, a lady stepped to the front of the room and welcomed everyone, asking if they'd bow their heads in prayer.

Seth obliged and prayed his own silent prayer: *God, this thing with my earpieces is a miracle within itself but I pray too now for another miracle: Please give me the words to say to these people here.*

AMEN. All opened their eyes and looked at Seth.

7

The words just fell from his lips. Seth went on for about 20 minutes about music and God. He spoke of how they all have a song inside that they need to express. He spoke of how God longs to hear those words. He then quoted some scripture (much to his surprise) about how God quietens them with his love and rejoices over them with singing.

"Imagine that! The God of the universe singing a song over us." Seth declared enthusiastically. There were a few

28

"Amens" and nods of approval that followed. Seth felt exhilarated and was buzzing inside. Once the service concluded he was approached by a middle-aged couple.

"Want to go for a drink?" the man asked with a smile. Seth glanced up at the clock on the wall. 10:30am. *A little too early for a drink.* Where Seth was from, having a drink that early on a Sunday seemed like a crime. Seth and the couple arrived at a local pub called *The Swan by the Water* - they followed the path that ran alongside the canal. Seth took in his surroundings, noting how some people lived on the canal in rather comfortable looking boats. These water homes were well equipped - gas bottles for cooking, table and chairs, a bucket, clothesline, drying rack, pots and pans, spotlight, pot plants, ornaments, garden gnomes – whole lives there, on a boat.

The friendly couple and Seth found a vacant table outside. While they waited to be served, they basked in the English sunshine. When his pint of beer arrived, Seth asked if they could charge his iPod behind the bar counter. The waitress obliged. Before taking a drink, Seth noticed how the sunlight shone through the beer displaying an enticing golden colour. The sun hung overhead, and Seth felt so blissful.

"Cheers! To perfect little moments." The man toasted.

"That string together adding to the journey of life." His wife added.

Later that day, after waving his goodbyes, Seth sat in the car and switched on the fully charged iPod waiting for the song to conclude. *Where will I end up next?*

8

The next song was Please Come Home by Dustin Kensrue and with the same familiar FLASH, VERY LOUD NOISE AND PITCH DARKNESS, RECOVERED LIGHT... Seth found himself sitting on a park bench. The weather felt a lot warmer. The bite in the air had disappeared. He took in his surroundings - he was in some sort of park. He took off his bag (aware of the length of the song). Leaving it on the bench, he decided to try and find an information board, so he could work out where he was. He followed a path that was bordered by daffodils and daisies. The orchestra of insects and birds seem to be at full volume as they buzzed and darted around from bush to bush. The garden certainly teemed with life. A few metres away he came across a board. Protea Park. He was in Pretoria in South Africa. He had once heard about this park through a cousin of his.

Just then, Seth had to react quickly and duck as a frisbee almost hit him. Hearing the distant apologies, Seth replied, "No worries, isn't this day just so beautiful!" and threw the frisbee back with precise elevation and distance.

He headed back to the bench and opened the packet of biscuits from his bag. Seth also wanted to take stock and write notes of his adventure and decided to jot down some thoughts in the notebook he had brought along. He opened the book. Strewn across two pages were quotes that he himself didn't write, but the words pulled him in:

"I live in a very small house, but my windows look out on a very large world." - Confucius 550-478 B.C.

"And now here is my secret, a very simple secret: It is only with the heart that one can see rightly; what is essential is invisible to the eye." — Antoine de Saint-Exupéry

The quotes were so appropriate for him. He needed to read those words and then to live out their inspiration. Consequently, he declared on that bench that he would live each moment from that day onwards with a wide-eyed wonder. Even if that required seeing things from his heart. Despite the heat swarming around him, Seth felt a coolness within. He felt like he was in the right place at the right time - a sort of inner peace, if you will. *Where to next?*

He looked to the iPod and counted down the last few seconds to the next song. Just before it ended, he glanced at his surroundings one last time.

FLASH.
BRIGHT LIGHT. WHISSHH!!
PITCH DARK.
RECOVERING LIGHT.

9

The first thing he noticed was the cobbled stones. The road that meandered before him was part of a quaint little town. He wondered where he was. He sang along to the chorus that now played, a song by Thrice: In Exile.

He walked on slowly enchanted by the old buildings that stood tall and proud alongside the road. He imagined the history that each brick carried. He noted a sign on one of the buildings sporting the name of the town: Lemgo, Germany. There was a feeling of festivity about the town. A couple walked by, laughing, hand in hand. Red flowers peeked from their pots on the balcony of a first-floor apartment. A little boy giggled as he put his hands in the spray of the fountain in the middle of the town square. The smell of Bratwurst hovered, enticing curious tourists to wait in line at the food stalls. Seth felt giddy. He continued to amble slowly through the town, up some streets, down some alley ways and across some parks. It was near the edge of town, where he heard the faint music coming from a church. *And what a magnificent church it was.* The spire seemed to poke a hole in the clouds above. The wooden entrance doors were like the ones of an ancient fort. As he neared the building, he had to turn the volume of his iPod down to zero, even removing his earpieces. The music coming from inside drew him in.

He slipped through the large doors that had been left ajar from the previous visitor. The organ pipes loomed over the golden altar in front of the sanctuary. He could smell the old wood of the church pews. There was an elderly lady playing the organ with reckless abandon, the sound reverberating through the organ pipes, right through Seth's skin to his very insides. *If only I could freeze this moment.*

He restarted the song, so he could stay longer. The stained glassed windows invited the sunlight in, displaying incredible colours sprinkled across the sanctuary floor. Blue, green and orange. Seth could smell some incense. As the song continued, he looked at the visitors who arrived after him - he could *see* how the music seemed to strip off the anxiety from their shoulders. Silent prayers of gratitude spilled from their lips. *What a beautiful moment!*

Pensively, he walked out, the song now had only 15 seconds left. He put the earpieces back in. Where would he end up next?

10

FLASH.
BRIGHT LIGHT. WHISSHH!!
PITCH DARK.
RECOVERING LIGHT.

Next up was a song by Relient K: The Lining Is Silver
Seth hurriedly put the volume down. He was in some sort of viewing hut. There was a watering hole ahead of him. He grabbed the binoculars in front of him and peered out – there was so much life out there: zebra and buffalo were drinking, and various birds darted to and fro in front of the bird hide. He spotted: Glossy Starlings, Speckled Mouse Birds, a Kurrichane Thrush and even a Malachite Kingfisher. Seth gathered that he was in some sort of game reserve. He instinctively grabbed the flask of coffee in front of him. As he was about to take sip:

"Sure, go ahead, you may have some of my coffee. Do you want a snack with that too?"
Seth blushed. "Aaagh, I'm sorry. I just thought..."
She smiled. "Hi, I'm Myrah. You are?"
"Seth."
"Isn't this just so beautiful?"
But her voice zoned out as Seth noticed her beautiful auburn-brown eyes. Her wavy black hair flowed down below her shoulders. Her voice became audible again.
"You didn't hear everything I said, did you?" She teased.
He blushed again. "Oops, busted."
Others in the hut *shooed* them out because they were talking a little too loudly. There was a beep and Seth looked down noticing that the battery on his iPod was about to die. But he didn't mind, he wanted to stay there longer with this intriguing and lovely girl. Myrah invited him to join her by the pool in the campsite entertainment area. He asked the waiter to charge his iPod as he ordered two ciders. Seth and Myrah sat with their feet dangling in the pool.

"Africa has the most beautiful sunsets."

33

It was more of a statement than a conversation starter. The silence that followed wasn't uncomfortable. They both looked out to the edge of the camp as the sun slowly sank beneath the treeline. A red glow filled the air. It was a wonderful night. Seth and Myrah shared their many stories. Their childhood, their dreams and their interests. Neither of them wanted to admit upfront but they both really enjoyed the other's company. The stars glimmered keenly as if they were listening in on their conversation. Seth proceeded to tell Myrah about the mystery man who gave him the "magical iPod." He shared some of the places he had been - the crashing into the snow, the powerful piece of music in Germany and the crispness of the English air. He even mentioned the sermon he preached. She stared at him mouth-gaping. Seth smiled at her and reached to close her mouth. She blushed.

"I'm not crazy, you know?"

She nodded. Words failed her.

"Let me show you." He requested his iPod back from the waiter. Put on his backpack. And then reached out for her hand. Myrah held it. He noticed how soft and warm her hands were and felt a little skip inside his heart. He pressed PLAY. The Relient K song was ending. Then it happened.

11

FLASH.
BRIGHT LIGHT. WHISSHH!!
PITCH DARK.
RECOVERING LIGHT.

But no Myrah. Only the warmth of her hand lingered in his palm. He tried to select the previous song again. It was

34

not on the iPod anymore. His heart sank. *What just happened?*

Kings of Leon – Back down South played quietly in his ears. Seth was dejected. He just sat there, eyes closed, not caring where he was. He wiped a tear from his cheek. *How can this be? How can I miss her so? I just met her.* But it felt as if he had known her for a long time. He then recalled something she said: "I love receiving hand-written letters."

He opened his eyes and took out his notebook. On the next empty page, he began to write:

Dear Myrah,

I don't even know how to start this. I cried when I arrived this side. I wish you could be here. I wish I could stay there in the bush camp with you. I feel so stupid that my attempt to bring you on an adventure didn't work.

And now, where would I even send this letter? I know you said you like receiving handwritten letters. So that's what this letter is, although I don't know if you will ever receive it but writing it makes me feel connected to you.

I am in Italy now at a beach town called Sorrento. It's stunning!

There is a glimmer on the ocean as if someone has thrown a whole bunch of diamonds in the water.

I fear that I may never see you, but I hope to God that's not true.

I even tried playing the same song to get back to you, but the song isn't on the iPod anymore. I've noticed that once a song has been played it "magically" disappears off the device.

I don't know exactly how to explain how I feel. I am very new to this sort of thing, but I know I miss you and I want you here with me. I want you to see what I see. Better still, I want to see things together and talk about them.

Will I see you again? I don't know. I can only hope and pray.

Thank you for a magical time under the African sky.

Yours truly,
Seth

12

He restarted the song four times as he wrote. At the end of the letter he added the date. By now Seth realised the PAUSE button didn't work anymore - he could only restart a song or wait for the next one. And the other scenario would be that of the battery going flat. And right now, that's what he wanted. The Mediterranean Sea invited him in. He kept repeating the Kings of Leon song till the battery died by the which time he knew all the words to Back Down South.

Now he was temporarily "stuck" in Italy. To clear his mind of the sadness he felt, he thought that a swim would be a good remedy. He found a little hiding place for his backpack behind a pot-plant on a deserted street. He used some of his cash to buy swimming shorts. Strangely, again, the currency in his wallet had switched to Euros. *All of this is very bizarre! But I am going to enjoy this crazy adventure and not question too much, rather just roll with it.*

The water seemed to saturate right through to his bones. It was bliss, it was a sort of baptism. He felt revived. Yes, he still missed Myrah, but he would hold on to hope, because that was all he could do. He saw an abandoned barge that was about two hundred metres from the shore and decided he would swim for that. As he headed for it, he submerged under the water, opened his eyes and took in the underwater paradise. Seaweed danced in the current below, shoals of fish swimming by. He couldn't identify them but that didn't matter - sometimes beauty doesn't need a name.

Later that day, he craved some ice-cream, so he got himself some chocolate Gelato – it seemed fitting to have that in its birthplace. He managed to find a place to charge the iPod. Seth was feeling tired, so he searched for a local park where he could have a little siesta. (*You know, when in Europe – do European things.*) He awoke a while later, ready for his next destination. He switched on his iPod and pressed PLAY.

FLASH.
BRIGHT LIGHT. WHISSHH!!
PITCH DARK.
RECOVERING LIGHT.

13

"I can ride my bike with no handlebars, no handlebars, no handlebars"

How fitting! Those were the words in his ears as he realised he was busy cycling – somewhere that *seemed rather flat?* He still needed to work out his exact location. He smiled to himself noticing how fresh the air was. *Gosh, I haven't heard this Flobots song in ages.* In the distance he saw a windmill. That was the clue he needed. He remembered from Geography lessons that Holland was a rather flat country sprinkled with windmills and flowers. Seth noted how light his soul felt in that place. Holland is a small country, but it seemed so spacious with the vast farmlands that decorate it.

Further down the road he collided with the beautiful aroma of freshly roasted coffee. *When did I last have coffee?* He decided to stop in for a cup. It was a quaint little coffee shop. The barista's English carried an American accent. He offered him a *stroopwafel* with the coffee. The small waffle was placed on the rim of the mug. The warmth of the coffee melted the syrup inside. The delicious waffle crumbled in his mouth. *Wow!*

Seth took in his surroundings:
I really should do this more often. His thoughts continued... *A lot of small beautiful moments happen around each person and how often, I and probably they, miss it.*
He looked at the iPod. There were about eleven songs left. Just then, an idea popped into his head. *I really should keep some mementos of each place I have visited.* He walked into a local curio shop and decided he would start a collection of fridge magnets. He found a perfect one for this Holland adventure. It was a pair of clogs leaning against a windmill. Seth also ended up buying a shirt - the one he had was well worn. After putting the fresh one on he decided to explore some more. He restarted the song again. That action was becoming second nature to him.
It wasn't the best song to have on repeat. "I can ride my bike with no handlebars..."
He discovered a long canal that he rode alongside. There were trees aligned on both sides that went on for as long as the eye could see. As he rode along the paving, he could feel the sunlight chopping through him as it came through the gaps in the trees. Seth noticed he had started observing and enjoying the smallest of life's pleasures. He knew it would be something he would carry on even after the iPod adventure had concluded.

14 (Myrah)

The silence of the stars hung above her. The night seemed quieter than usual. She wondered if she had just imagined this all. She heard the distant *toot-toot* of a Spotted Eagle owl. The chill of the evening air clashed with the warmth she felt inside. She knew she had only just met him. But she really did enjoy his company. Dare she admit that she even liked him? But now what? He's gone!

I can't believe how sad I feel. She held her hand in a fist. She didn't want the warmth of his hand to escape. Myrah mulled over the story Seth had shared with her - the seemingly magical iPod.

Did it really take him to all those places? It seemed so impossible, but he was here and now he was not. She didn't have a piece of paper or pen with her, but she needed to gather her thoughts. She decided to speak out to the night-time sky. Even if he would never hear her words, the sky would soak them in. *All people live under the same sky, right?* She lay on her back and started with her spoken poem:

> "I wish time could stand still
> Your hand in mine, such a thrill
> How I wish a song would bring you
> Back, here under the starlit sky, me and you
>
> Will I see you again?
> I know it's crazy, call me insane
> But I miss you already
> I wonder where in the world you are now.
>
> I throw my heart in these words
> I throw them in the sky
> I hope they will land on your path
> This sonnet is my SOS cry."

She wiped her tears, stood up and headed back for the tent where her family were staying. She knew she must hold on to hope and be thankful, even for the short magical time she had with Seth. Life is a mystery - she knew that now.

15 (Seth)

FLASH.
BRIGHT LIGHT. WHISSHH!!
PITCH DARK.
RECOVERING LIGHT.

As Seth opened his eyes, he realised he was whizzing down a slide. Far from being in a water park, he instead found himself in a store that sold winter gear from ski jackets, to snowboards, to beanies, to thick coats and scarves. The slide was an attempt to add a fun and hip factor to retail. So, there he was, dressed warmly, composing himself after the slide. In front of him, chuckling, were a guy and two girls. The song that played in his ears was one by Counting Crows: Anna Begins. (Ironically, it turned out that one of the girls' names was Anna.) She nudged Seth in his side and asked:

"Why do you have your earphones in?"

Seth felt a tinge of guilt and removed one earpiece. The question on hand was to work out where he was. The three friends invited Seth to join them and then headed out of the store. He followed, stepped outside and was met by a fresh, cool breeze - the chill of nearby snow. Seth glanced at a nearby information board and saw the name of the town. He was in Reykjavik, the capital of Iceland.

His general knowledge reminded him that the Northern Lights can be seen from this beautiful country. He hoped he'd get to see them... if his current adventure allowed it...

Tony, the other guy in the party of four grabbed him by the arm and said:

"Let's go do something crazy!" and winked at him. The girls said they'd go shopping. Seth ran after Tony as he headed for the nearby bay.

"Have you ever swum in the Rauðavatn Lake?"

"Nope, but I'm going to beat you to it." Seth stripped down to his boxers and ran for the water. The cold ran right through their bodies, but they felt so alive at the same time.

"Brrr, this is insane! But so awesome!"

Later that evening around 9pm, they were all sitting on a bus, going to look for the Northern Lights. Seth was consumed with excitement and forgot to restart the song.

FLASH.
BRIGHT LIGHT. WHISSHH!!
PITCH DARK.
RECOVERING LIGHT.

16

It had been a great afternoon in Belgium. Seth had found a quaint coffee shop whose tables and chairs spilled out onto a cobblestoned sidewalk. He was sitting there with his journal open - the aroma of the cappuccino relaxed him. He decided he wanted to share more of his adventures with Myrah, so he wrote another letter. He restarted the song by Anberlin: Northern Lights. (A cheeky song title that took him away from Iceland before he ever got to see them.) It was the seventeenth time he had restarted that song. If there was another thing he'd gained from the mysterious iPod adventure, it would be knowing all those songs off by heart!

And isn't that the beauty of music, he mused - *A song can always take you to another time and another place.* "Music is powerful. It can transport you."

He ordered his third waffle, next trying the caramel and Oreo topping. *I'm in the "capital of chocolate" – I might as well indulge.*

He wrote:

I think I'm suffering from a sugar rush. Okay maybe "suffering" is not the right word, haha! I am writing from Belgium - I'm in Bruges now, sitting at a coffee shop and writing to you. When I "landed" here I ended up in a canal boat.

It was incredible to see the city from that level. If there is anything that this "magical iPod adventure" has taught and shown me, is that there are so many beautiful and unusual things all over the world. Also, in each place, there are ordinary people doing ordinary things which in itself seems kind of extra-ordinary. Let me explain:

After the canal boat ride, I decided to just amble around the streets. I wanted to get "lost" in a sense and walk with no agenda. So, I kept walking, not taking notice of any landmarks, (besides if I were really stuck and worried, I would have just waited for the iPod to go to the next song. Then I'd be "found" again, just in a new place.)

I saw a couple lying together on a blanket in a park, they were reading together and sharing lines from their book with one another. I saw an elderly man pick a flower and give it to his wife; a young boy throwing a Frisbee for his dog. I watched a businessman sip on coffee and soak in the moment - he seemed so content.

A taxi driver got out his car, helped a passenger into his vehicle and loaded the boot. (I know it is part of his job - but still his actions moved me)

I noticed a young girl thoroughly enjoying her waffle. I could tell since she had sauce, syrup and topping all over her lips, cheeks, and fingers!

Two pigeons were courting, the male doting on the female.

I saw a student walking with conviction to the local campus. He seemed so determined – hinting that he was either late or excited about his next class.

In another direction, I spotted a lady who wore a summer dress – she was on her bicycle: as she free-wheeled, she stretched out her arms as if she were flying, chopping the air with her arms.

All these ordinary actions by ordinary people were simply stunning to witness!

I miss you,
Seth

FLASH.
BRIGHT LIGHT. WHISSHH!!
PITCH DARK.
RECOVERING LIGHT.

17

The next song Seth heard was by Dead Poetic. He had heard a few of their songs before and loved their lyrics. They were honest and made you think. *That's how music really should be.*

This song was called: "The Dreamclub Murderers." As he arrived in the next scene, he was overcome with the coolness in the air. The ground was covered in a white blanket of snow. Its chill pierced through his jeans. He put on his hoodie and beanie and decided to take out his camera too. Seth found himself in a wooded area. The tall bare trees loomed over him – it looked as if they were stuck in the snow. There was a sort of charm about the place. Seth felt like he was a writer pondering his next novel and sensed his inspiration would come from that place. He peered out of the wooded area and noticed the glossy surface of the nearby road. The melted snow made for dangerous driving conditions. The cars slowed their pace. From the road signs, he was able to work out where he was: Warsaw. He gazed out to the city buildings in the distance. *This is so cool. I'm in Poland!*

The song that played ended with these lyrics: "So sleep child, no one can touch you now, no one can hurt you now, not here, anymore." Automatically, he restarted the song.

He had learnt a bit about Warsaw from history classes when he was in primary school which had covered World Wars I and II. Although over fifty years since this place was ruined by the war, the weather of that day added a certain gloom to the city. *Sometimes the sadness of history never leaves a place. And the weather certainly doesn't help.*

He turned his attention back to the wooded area. Its charm remained but he felt a shiver go down to his bones. He headed for a nearby coffee shop. Not knowing any Polish, Seth just pointed to the picture of the coffee on the display menu. The barista behind the counter understood and smiled back at him, then headed off to go and make it. Seth felt a little under-dressed as all the locals were wearing coats. He decided there and then to buy one too.

The coat will serve as a great souvenir when I'm back home. That was the first time he thought of home, and he didn't even miss it. Although he did wonder how time worked on this adventure. Was it running parallel to the real world or not? In the end, he decided not to ponder too much but just roll with it. The barista brought hot chocolate instead. *Okay, so maybe she didn't understand my order*, but the mistake worked out great. He took a sip and smiled in appreciation. The chocolate in the drink tasted so delicious that he wondered if it was made with Wedel chocolate. Oh, so heavenly! He restarted the song.

The neighbouring store sold coats. The one he purchased had a thick strip of fur on the collar that kept his neck warm. He continued to the woods. Earlier he had seen a bench that he wanted to sit on. Using the sleeve of his arm, he wiped away the accumulated fallen snow. He then sat and listened.

He heard the faint rustling of the leaves up above from a very slight breeze and he noticed a robin hopping from branch to branch a few metres away. *I wonder if birds like the snow.*

He decided to take a little stroll and as he trudged on could feel the moisture slowly seeping through his shoes. He walked on through a graveyard - there were some war memorials that had been put up. *No one wins in war.*

18

FLASH.
BRIGHT LIGHT. WHISSHH!!
PITCH DARK.
RECOVERING LIGHT.

"If you give, you begin to live. You might die trying."

A song by Dave Matthews Band greeted him and he smiled at the familiarity - it was his favourite band. That next scene had him "jump" across the border to Germany: Berlin. He had arrived in front of the Berlin Wall. It was warmer there – only a few patches of snow lay around, the rest had melted. He saw a local market and decided to amble among the stalls. He came across a stall selling Glühwein; *when in Rome, do as the Romans do. Same in Germany, right?*

He ordered a glass and sipped slowly - the warmth of the drink took away his remaining shivers. Seth had heard from his friend, Clayton, about an artistic structure nearby. He'd go and take pictures so that one day when they met up again, he would be able to show that he too had been there.

That thought came with a tinge of loneliness - he missed his friend and he missed Myrah, although he didn't miss home yet - he was still loving the adventure he was on.

He found the structure: Molecular Man - an aluminium sculpture of three men with hundreds of holes throughout their bodies, representing the molecules of humans that bring them into existence. The *aluminium men* appeared to be throwing high fives to one another. While he was snapping away with his camera, he heard a familiar voice:

"Seth is that you? What on earth..."

He swung around. "Clayton, oh my goodness!"

After hugs and laughter, Seth said, "I was taking pictures as proof, to show you that I too had been here."

"Wh...what are you doing here? Two nights ago, we were skyping, and you never mentioned anything about coming here."

"I have a very strange but amazing story to tell you - and I also need to charge this iPod, please? It's related to my strange story!" Clayton looked at his watch.

"I have to finish my shift. How about I direct you to my flat, I have a docking station there? Perhaps you can freshen up too, looks like you need it." He laughed. "But... wait, how are long are you here for?"

"As long as I like. I get to choose." Seth replied. "I will explain later."

"Cool man, sounds good." Clayton handed over his flat keys and gave him directions to his place. As he headed off for work, he shouted back, "Tonight we grab some beers from the Hard Rock Café that you told me about."

"Definitely!" They parted ways - Seth felt happy, this adventure "allowed" him to share a part of it with his good friend. *Adventures are to be shared.*

19

Clayton's apartment overlooked the city hub. The city centre was teeming with activity: street entertainers, Glühwein vendors, coffee shops and a few curio stores. There was also a tram track that ran through the west side of the town square.

The docking station was a snazzy one! Instead of Seth having to restart the song every time, he pressed the repeat button on the docking station. He then turned the volume low - he didn't want "to kill" his favourite band.

He felt the tiredness overcome him, so he showered and then had a nap - falling asleep to the thought of that wonderful night with Myrah under the African sky.

(Clayton)

Clayton's shift went by quickly with the questions racing in his head: *What is Seth doing here? I spoke to him online less than two days ago and now he is in Germany. And what's with that iPod and the need to charge it?* He was keen to get some answers, but better still he was excited to have that beer and burger and a good catch up with his friend.

(Seth)

Clayton's knock woke Seth. After putting his work bag down, Clayton made them a pot of tea. Then the conversation just flowed from one thing to another: their latest hobbies, their recent album purchases and some recent comical moments.

8pm.

They caught the tram to the other side of town. *Public transport is so cool.* Seth thought. *Signs of a first world country.*

The illuminated sign made him beam – there they were, at the entrance of a Hard Rock Café. Seth had always wondered what it would be like to visit one of these café's scattered all over the world. And here he was having his first HRC experience in Berlin with his good mate. *Life has such beautiful moments!*

"Woohoo! Let's do this. First round on me." Again, his wallet had euros in it. *Hmm, I wonder who is funding this magical adventure.* He shrugged and thought: *Less questions and more living.*

20

They sat under a guitar that Jimi Hendrix used on a European tour back in the 60's. The pint of Kölsch seemed to glisten in the dimly lit booth.

"What are you doing here? How did you get to Germany?" Clayton probed.

Seth went on to tell him about the mystery man who visited him in the music store - dropping off the iPod. He shared his mantra: "Music is powerful... it can transport you." Clayton smiled in agreement. He went on to tell him about how each song magically "took him" to another place.

"What places have you seen?"

"Bruges, Reykjavik, Sorrento, Morzine, Silverstone..."

"Silverstone?"

"Yeah, in the UK. I even got to preach there."

"For real?"

"Yeah man, I totally owned it - I spoke about music and related that to God."

He shared the various experiences in each country he had visited. Clayton had the same reaction as Myrah - he sat there astonished!

"How on earth is this possible?"

"I have no clue! But I have stopped questioning it and just rolling with it. I have only a handful of songs left - I think?"

Clayton ordered another round when the burgers came. They had ordered the HRC special: two huge patties, smothered in barbecue and cheese sauce – with a slice of pineapple and some French fries too.

"The sad thing though is that I met a girl along the way and well, now she's gone. I was telling her about the iPod and I wanted to show her - to take her with me to the *next stop.*"

He told Clayton all about the magical time with Myrah, their inspiring conversation and the vast canopy of stars above them.

"So, you just met this girl and were going to whisk her away to another place..." Clayton smirked.

Seth chuckled. "Yeah, I know it's crazy, but everything about this iPod adventure is so surreal! We were both just so lost in the moment and decided to just try!" Seth explained to Clayton how they held hands thinking that that connection would be enough for them to be 'transported together'.

A silenced landed between the two friends. They sipped their beers in the stillness.

"Maybe if you each had one earpiece in one of your ears, the 'transporting' would have worked, because it's the iPod that is the 'magical thing,' right?"

Seth jumped up in excitement. And then sat back down. "Wow, dude, you're a genius! That makes so much sense." Then he shrugged. "But now I will never know."

49

"Chin up dude, hope is a beautiful thing. I believe you will meet her again. All things are possible"
The optimism fell on the table between them.
"Let's get dessert," Seth suggested.

Clayton shook his head. He couldn't believe his friend's luck. The magical iPod. It was all so incredible! Ironically, a song by the Beatles played on the restaurant's sound system "I wanna hold your hand..." *Well clearly, that didn't work with Myrah.* Seth smiled to himself. *But yes, hope is a beautiful thing. Clayton is right.*

21

It was 11:45pm when they got back.
"Should we try out the one earpiece thing?" Seth suggested.
Clayton hesitated. You could see he was working through a thought process: "Seth, I don't think we should, my reason being that maybe the 'earpiece' trick only works once. And if that's the case, you should use it on the girl. Myrah sounds amazing!"
Seth nodded in agreement. He knew too that the iPod didn't go back to the same 'scene' and once the song had played it got deleted automatically - *how would Clayton get back to Berlin?*
Clayton continued: "Use it wisely my friend. You and I have many more adventures lined up regardless of the iPod."
That night Seth bunked on Clayton's couch. He faintly heard that Dave Matthew's song play in the background. *This song must have repeated over a hundred times by now.* In the morning, Seth would move on to to the next song and into the next scene. He couldn't fall asleep right away, so

he decided to write another letter to Myrah. He wrote about his time with Clayton and shared his suggestion about the earpiece and he also told her about Warsaw. He closed his journal, zipped up the sleeping bag and fell asleep.

In the morning they had breakfast and then exchanged farewells. Seth gave Clayton a bracelet he bought in Sorrento. "For you. Thanks so much for a great time! My brother-in-arms."

Clayton smiled at the familiar phrase and replied, "I can't wait to meet Myrah."

Seth pressed NEXT SONG
FLASH.
BRIGHT LIGHT. WHISSHH!!
PITCH DARK.
RECOVERING LIGHT.

22

"I cannot live, I cannot breathe, unless you do this with me," repeated over in his head as Seth found himself sitting comfortably in a train. *I wonder where I'm headed.*

Just then the train announcer spoke: "Northbound train to Leeds, next stop Derby - please take all your luggage with you." *Hmm, what will I be doing there?*

Just then, the lady next to him said "Excuse me, young man, you seemed to have dropped your ticket." She handed it over. "Thank you," he replied. The destination on the ticket was Ilkley. *So, Leeds is not my end point.* He asked the conductor how he was to get to Ilkley and how much longer the journey was. The conductor explained which platform Seth should look for in Leeds and then said with a smile, "And you have another hour or so. Enjoy the journey. The scenery out there is beautiful!"

She was right! He became aware of the passing views. With his head leaning against the window he peered out and found he was thoroughly enjoying himself. *The English countryside is a spectacular thing to witness. There is a diversity and dreaminess to it all.* Seth remembered a book he had read about a year back called *The Unlikely Pilgrimage of Harold Fry*. He was now seeing a lot of that countryside imagery in real life. He saw the daffodils swaying to and fro. He saw various country lanes meandering into the distance. The sheep grazing on the small hills. The green abundance of the landscape. It was all so picturesque.

He remembered a quote from that book, about how life looks quite different from ground level when you're on your feet. Too often, people in cars skim past many beautiful ordinary things, same could be said for trains - however as a passenger, one has the option to take in the scenery, if they choose to do that. The man who sat across him didn't - the affairs of the world seemed more important as he had his nose lost in the local paper. Seth noticed a large splash of orange on the cover and read a headline about Blackpool being promoted. He wondered if there was ever a newspaper without any football news.

Briefly, Seth observed the others in the coach too. A teenage girl was engrossed in her phone - her fingers seemed to be playing hopscotch on the keypad. A businessman wore a frown on his face as he typed away on his laptop. Perhaps it was a last-minute report he had to complete or amend. An elderly lady was happily engaged in her needlework. It looked to Seth that she was making some mittens. The sweetest thing he noticed was a couple who sat huddled together: they angled their bodies to look out the window, each holding a book. He was reading a Wilbur Smith and she was reading one of the classics. They were lost in the moment, their gaze shifting between the outside world, the words on the page and each other's eyes. If there ever was a moment to freeze frame, that would be it.

23

Again, he restarted the song. He did another thorough search hoping for a REPEAT SONG option - but to no avail - that *old-school* iPod had no such function.

Time seemed to move slowly. It was as if that part of the adventure was planned: the sitting, his racing thoughts as the scenery zipped by and the unexpected emotions swimming to the surface. An alliteration formed in his mind: People. Places. Present.

Outside he noticed the landscaping changing: first the wildness of the Dales, then the many little farms bordered with limestone walls – making the land look like a giant checkers board – and finally the heather cloaked moors. It was so picturesque! The alliteration invaded his thoughts again. Those three things he knew were important to him:

Present – This mysterious adventure was teaching him that. From the conversation he overheard in Silverstone between the mom and her son, to the tug of war of attention between his thoughts of Myrah and being present in each place he visited. For him, to be present was to savour the taste of a good beer, smell the aroma of good coffee and to allow a view to take your breath away. In fact, to use all one's five senses in each moment; he remembered his recent visit to Sorrento – the sound of the rhythmic waves lapping the sand, seeing the glistening surface of the sea, hearing the gulls and the people enjoying themselves, smelling the sea air and tasting the salt water when he swam.

53

Places – Now he knew the thrill of seeing and experiencing new places. From simply having an ice cream on the beach or seeing the snow-capped mountains for as far as the eye could see – this adventure had afforded him such an appreciation for both ordinary and extraordinary places. Beauty can be found in every place.

People – Life needs to involve people. He thought of the people he had met thus far in his few years: from best friends, to the recent Myrah and of course, his own family. He then thought of how his dad inspired good values such as gratitude, optimism, and wanderlust. He thought of how it would be good to visit one of these places with his dad. *If only.*

24

FLASH.
BRIGHT LIGHT. WHISSHH!!
PITCH DARK.
RECOVERING LIGHT.

He never made it to Ilkley. He had forgotten to restart the song. He felt a tinge of disappointment but not for long. *Perhaps that was the point of the train trip – travelling with my thoughts.*

He held his breath as he took in the incredible scenery that lay before him. *The hills are alive with the sound of music.* Seth thought. Although that wasn't the song he heard through his earpiece. *Where am I?*

"Oh, what a fix they're in, Oh, what a terrible sin, Oh, what a fix they're in, Oh, what a terrible sinister game." the woman sang. Glancing at the display, the artist was Dear Reader. Their music had an indie folk feel – the song about a great white bear. Homing in on the words, he felt the song was about facing one's fears.

Focusing on his surroundings again, still unaware of where he was - he ambled across some small stones to the water's edge. The water was cold. He picked up a pebble and lobbed it into the distance. As it pierced the water the surface exhibited concentric circular ripples that spread far out. It seemed as if that was the first disturbance the water had experienced all day. In the distance, he saw a sign at the water's edge. *The name of the dam must be on there.* He headed for it. It was a tourist information board:

Dear Traveller,
You have heard the legend
You have wondered if it were true
Now gaze into the abyss
And wait for me to show my head.
The Loch Ness Monster

Wow, I am in Scotland! He thought back to his primary school days – to his geography teacher mentioning the Loch Ness Monster and now here he was - standing at the edge of Loch Ness. *This is so surreal!*

Then the urge hit him, the craving for some afternoon tea - a very British thing to do. Although he was in Scottish territory the sentiment was the same! *Besides it's way too early for whisky!* Some distance alongside the loch he noticed a tearoom – he went and sat at a table that seem to peer over the water's edge. In her strong Scottish accent, a waitress greeted him and took his order. The tea arrived with a welcomed surprise: a scone with jam and cream.

He was disturbed by a familiar voice:

"Hi Seth, may I join you?"

Seth turned to see his dad walking towards him. It seemed he was expecting to meet Seth there at the tearoom.

"What a nice surprise that you are all the way this side of the world." His dad continued. Although confused, Seth stood up and gave him a hug. "Hi, Dad." *This adventure is full of surprises! And to think I was just thinking about him on the train.*

Seth ordered another tea for his dad, while his dad spoke about the train ride to Scotland from his hometown down south. His dad shared his surprise of receiving the email from Seth. Seth gazed at him, puzzled. His dad asked him:
"Why did you end the email with Mystery Man?" He then chuckled, "I even googled 'Mystery Man' to see if it was a new band you were into." He winked at his son, "You know you and your music, you are always thinking in lyrics and speaking of bands."
Seth nodded and shrugged, hoping that non-verbal cue would be a satisfactory answer for his dad. *Hmm*, so the nameless *"mystery man" had arranged this.* However, it was possible, Seth was pleased to be sharing that part of the adventure with his dad. He had some gratitude to express.

25

Seth thanked his dad for the life values he had passed on, such as appreciation for even the smallest things. He shared too about two of the recent places he visited. He wanted the story of his travels to sound plausible - there was no way he could tell his dad about the iPod and the mystery man. *Most adults struggle to believe in things like that.* Instead, he took out the earpiece and secretly restarted the song a few times till the battery died. *I'll find a way to recharge it later.*
They had a good time chatting and after two cups of tea they walked the nearby paths that meandered through the

mountains. They walked for about two hours with his dad taking many pictures along the way.

There was a lot to explore in the area – so they made the most of it. He and his dad explored the nearby castle and the fort on the other end of the loch. *I must put this iPod on charge. Perhaps the ticket office can help me out?*
At one of the turrets of the castle, Seth excused himself and head down to the entrance - they were willing to help and put the iPod on charge. Seth also paid for two tickets for a castle tour at 11:30 - he knew his dad would appreciate that. It was an interesting and informative tour. At some point, during a break in the tour, Seth decided to take a quick look at the photos he had taken so far of "this mysterious adventure." To his shock, he discovered that all the photos were gone! *What had happened to them?* He hadn't deleted any. But then it occurred to him that perhaps taking photos was not possible on this adventure. The word: *Present* popped into his mind. *I need to be fully present and just embrace each moment as I experience them.* He was a little sad that he wouldn't be able to share some picture memories with his friends and family. But then he thought that some stories are best told without showing pictures but allowing the hearer to use their imagination and create their own pictures. He decided to jot down lyrics from John Mayer in his notebook:

"Didn't have a camera by my side this time, hoping I would see the world with both my eyes, maybe I will tell you about it."

After the tour they collected his charged iPod and bade each other farewell. Filled with joy and gratitude for the time with his dad, Seth was ready to move on. *"Thank you, God!"* Seth whispered and skipped to the next song.

FLASH.
BRIGHT LIGHT. WHISSHH!!
PITCH DARK.
RECOVERING LIGHT.

26

In the next scene the air was thinner, he could feel that his breathing was laboured. Tired of his jeans, he changed in to his boardshorts. He noticed that he was standing in some open field and the grass was knee high. He saw a tiny frozen pool a few metres away. The sun's position suggested that it was around 10am. He ventured towards the frozen pool, water ran below the surface and on top was a thin layered sheet of ice. He picked it up and held it against the sunlight. The rays that shone through made a pretty rainbow effect on the ground. Then Seth threw the sheet of ice – as it landed, it shattered! *Boys will be boys.*

A little stream ran from the pool and Seth followed it. It was then that he noticed he wasn't standing in an open field - but actually he was on top of a mountain! The stream he followed led him to the edge. The water trickled over. He couldn't believe that he'd not noticed the blanket of clouds that lay from the mountain's edge to as far as the eye could see. He was literally above the clouds! *All people need to learn to look around more, without blinkers, including me!* Another lesson Seth could add to this adventure's education.

His setting came together: the little pool of water had frozen because of the altitude. He was on a mountain top surrounded by a vast blanket of cloud. He wondered where he was. *Could this be the Drakensburg mountains?* He then tuned into the song playing:

"I'm searching for the spirit of a great heart under African skies." It was Johnny Clegg. *I wonder if the song is a clue to my location.*

It seemed to Seth that he was living in the memories of someone else. It was as if the memories were linked to the iPod. Well, to the songs on it. His mantra about music transporting you came to mind again. *Perhaps the iPod had belonged to someone else or the mystery man himself?*

27 (Myrah)

It had been two days since she had met Seth. She was sitting in the back seat of her parents' car heading back to the concrete wilderness. The city of Johannesburg was quite a contrast to the reserve where they had spent the last few days. Myrah and her parents had been living in Johannesburg for twenty-three years. Her parents lived in the south and she lived in the west, in a small flat in a quieter suburb. The only thing she'd brag about in her neighbourhood was Carol's Corner Café. It was a quaint little coffee shop that sat literally on a corner. The tables spilled out onto the pavement. Lots of people met there for business meetings or just to read or for a chance to pause from the busyness. It was also a place where you felt great and creative things began.

Myrah liked her quiet life - although she was visited by those occasional dreams of travel. Since that night under the stars with Seth, she couldn't shake off the desire to see some more of the world. With him would be ideal but she wondered if their paths would ever cross again. Her heart ached. *I hope we meet again. I wish he told me where he was from. Then I could have started a search there?*

With ten minutes left, she continued to peer out the window as the hustle and bustle of the city pulled the car in

– soon their vehicle would be lost in the massive crowd of cars in the city. One would often feel like "one in a million" in that huge place. To find someone there would be like looking for a needle in a haystack. *If only I could send out a signal flare to Seth. A girl can but dream.* She had this sinking feeling if he ever did come and look for her – where would he start and how would he find her? *We didn't even exchange surnames!*

28 (Seth)

FLASH.
BRIGHT LIGHT. WHISSHH!!
PITCH DARK.
RECOVERING LIGHT.

As he 'arrived' - a big wave hit the front of the ferry and the spray splashed the front window – the lyrics that played then seemed fitting: "My soul is alive and so are you." A song by P.O.D.

He saw that some of the other passengers were hiding their faces in brown paper bags, feeling seasick. It took him a few minutes to work out that they had just left Calais in France and were crossing the English Channel heading towards Dover. He smiled. *Wow, I have always wanted to see the white cliffs of Dover.* Another memory of Geography class.

The captain announced that they had forty minutes to go. Feeling hungry, Seth sat at a table that had a front facing view and ordered some French fries and a coke. Some people shook their heads at him, wondering how he could eat on such a topsy-turvy trip. But Seth was thrilled and felt secure as the water bashed against the glass and on the front deck – he hadn't been on a ferry before. *All these new experiences!*

He decided he would write to Myrah, to share some more of the adventure with her. *I wish I could tell her these stories in person.* Whether or not he would see her again, the writing served as a good travel journal anyway. He decided to compile a list of the soundtrack to his mysterious and amazing adventure. He knew that in time he would listen to the songs again and be reminded of the various scenes he had 'landed' in – a new visual memory accompanying each song:

1) Straatligkinders – Die avontuur van n' hartbreek
2) Linkin Park – Shadow of the day
3) Taking Back Sunday – Summer, man
4) Dustin Kensrue – Please Come Home
5) Thrice – In Exile
6) Relient K – The lining is silver
7) Kings of Leon – Back Down South
8) Flobots -Handlebars
9) Counting Crows – Anna Begins
10) Anberlin – Northern Lights
11) Dead Poetic – Dreamclub Murderers
12) Dave Matthews Band – Die Trying
13) Angels & Airwaves – The Adventure
14) Dear Reader – Great White Bear
15) Johnny Clegg – Great Heart
16) P.O.D. – If you could see me now
17)

He left a space for the last song - he didn't want to write it down yet, it made things feel too final. He felt sad, the experience had been so surreal - he didn't want it to end.

Seth saw that they were almost in Dover and noticed that the iPod needed to be recharged. But he felt like being defiant and staying a little longer in the adventure. *I will stay awhile in Dover. I want to see those cliffs. And I will amble around the little port town and see what I can discover.* He had to restart the song once more only, then about a third way through, it died - and just then the captain announced that they had arrived: "Passengers first and then vehicles, please." *Oh, this ferry must be carrying cars too.*

29

Seth checked his wallet, he had over two hundred pounds in there. *I could stay the night. I'm going to take a stroll for as far as I can go along these cliffs.* He walked down what seemed to be the main road and read the signs of the businesses that lined the street. He was looking for a place to stay for the night. He wanted to freshen up and leave his bag and the iPod in the room while it charged.

ANCHORS AHOY. The name of the guesthouse was displayed above the door and just below that on a chalkboard he read: "Two vacant rooms left." The door was painted white. He pushed it open and immediately there was an ascent of forty-two stairs. (He had counted just because he was so surprised at such an unexpected entrance.) At the top, there stood a lonely reception desk, and on the counter, a bell waited to be rung. He obliged and about twenty seconds later an elderly lady appeared.

"Good day to you" she chirped. Her smile assured Seth that this was the perfect place to hide away from the world for a little while. She had a pleasant English accent that hadn't been tainted by tourists.

"Hi there, mam, I'd like a room for the night please"

"Sure, dearie; that will be thirty-five pounds." Seth paid her. "Room twenty-three. It's down the corridor. On the right."

He smiled back, "Thank you."

"Be sure to explore the cliffs. It stays light till eight thirty, so make the most of it!"

Seth nodded. "I definitely will" and headed off for his room. It was two in the afternoon. There was a lot of daylight left. *A nap right now would be helpful.* He noticed how tired he felt, understandably - he had been on the go non-stop for an uncertain length of time - he wasn't sure of what day it was or how many days the adventure had been. Each time a song pushed him to the next scene he'd land at a different time of day. *This is probably what jetlag feels like?* A while back, he had stopped trying to work out how long he had been gone for.

Seth decided to fluff up the pillow and sit up against the headboard. *I wonder what's inside the drawer of this bedside table. I'm going to say a Gideon's bible. They always have those in B&B's and hotel rooms.*

But he was wrong, instead he saw a book by Bill Bryson: Notes from a Small Island. He read the description on the back. *Hmm, what a fitting book for this island I find myself on. Perhaps I'll learn some things from this.*

30 (Myrah)

Myrah was back into the swing of things. Her life was going on as usual. But she carried a skip in her step. She had had a dream about her and Seth backpacking some of Europe together. The following day after that dream she started getting ready for the adventure. She bought herself a backpack. She started reading about places in Europe and she bought herself a travel journal. She was going to fill it up with the places she would like to see. She would fill it with interesting facts about every city. *Then on the next pay day, I'll invest in a little digital camera.* She also listed other things she would buy in time: a sleeping bag, a travel pillow and a mini first aid kit. She would be ready. *Our paths will meet again. I will keep this backpack packed and ready.* Hope is a wonderful thing!

31 (The Mystery Man)

Sometimes great stories need a little nudge! The mystery man had been watching both of their lives closely. He had grown quite fond of Seth and Myrah and he knew Seth had only one more song to go. He would have to intervene somehow. *However, Seth must not see my face again, otherwise my plan won't work.*

32 (Myrah)

Myrah took her lunch break at Carol's. She sat at her favourite table and pulled out her laptop and travel journal. She would transfer her research to the book. *There is just something authentic about carrying a physical book with travel notes and ideas. Laptops and the internet seem so bound by a greater system.* She knew when she'd leave on her travels, she would leave the laptop behind. *Less is more.*

Since Seth had named some bands that she had not heard of, she had decided to give some of them a listen - she enjoyed Relient K and Dustin Kensrue. She also like some songs by Taking Back Sunday. *What a great name for a band!* She'd jotted down the names of her new favourite songs on the inside cover:

If you believe me
New Again
Therapy
Please Come Home

33 (Seth)

There were teacups on the cover, a London taxi and one of those red telephone booths. *What a vibrant and interesting cover!* There were no chapter names in the book, but he spotted the name 'Calais' in the second line and the word 'Dover' on the fifth page. *It must be a sign. I just sailed in from Calais today and here I am in Dover.* Seth enjoyed life's little interesting coincidences and he always wanted to explore them further. *The universe presents some interesting moments! How you treat them is part of the beauty of life. I'll just read the first chapter for now then head off for the cliffs.* Seth chuckled to himself as he read these words about Dover from those first few pages:

'...Dover was not vastly improved by daylight, but I liked it. I liked its small scale and cosy air, and the way everybody said "Good morning" ...'

An unusual "tourist guide" book for this town. But armed with this quirky knowledge Seth felt ready to go and explore. He put on his windbreaker even though the sun was shining outside. *If there is one thing that can be predictable about England's weather is that rain is inevitable.*

He got up from the bed. The room was cosy. There was a maroon bedside rug beneath his feet and the lampshade was light brown with seashells faintly printed on it. The duvet was white with a red blanket folded at the end of the bed. The cupboards were white too - enough space to store clothes for a month's stay. *Perhaps people boarded here for lengthy business trips?*

There was also a dark brown chest of drawers that lay in front of the window which looked out onto the street. On the chest of drawers was one of those self-catering trays that you'd find in most accommodation establishments: tea sachets, coffee, sugar, milk sachets and a mini kettle. There was also a painting on one wall - it was of a lighthouse alongside the Dover cliffs.

He walked out the room, along the corridor, down the stairs and out onto the street. He looked left and right. To the right was a pie shop called Greggs. Feeling hungry, Seth bought a Cornish pasty. He then headed back from the direction he had come and walked towards the cliffs. There was a pathway that looped upwards to them on the east side of the harbour.

34 (The Mystery Man)

He knew where the next song would take Seth. He would intercept him in that great city. With roughly eight million people he could easily do the "drop off" undetected. He knew Seth must not see him otherwise the mysterious adventure would come to an end instantly. *The main character of a story should never meet the story creator.* The mystery man was satisfied with his thoughts. *I think there is something in the ancient scriptures that is quite similar: 'But, He said, "You cannot see my face, for no one may see me and live."'* The mystery man knew his own place - he was no god, but the "adventure" that Seth was experiencing was of his creation and he wanted to alter the ending. Because Myrah was an unexpected twist in the tale...

35 (Myrah)

Myrah loved her apartment. It was a creative and safe place away from the chaos and noise of the world. She had a blackboard mounted up in her work room - it took up the whole wall. On it she scribbled her ideas, quotes and other interesting trivia she discovered. She decided to add some of the places and things she was keen on seeing with Seth. She felt a little obsessed, but Myrah had this gut feeling... *call it my sixth sense?* that she would cross paths with him again. She grabbed some yellow chalk and starting writing:

The beautiful city of Oxford
Hot-Air-Ballooning
The Sistine Chapel
Killarney in Ireland
Barcelona

36 (Seth)

"All right, mate?" a man walking down the path asked Seth.

"Yes, thank you." Seth wondered if it looked like he was struggling. *Odd, I feel fit and fine.*

A few hundred metres later the path flattened out a bit and it happened again:

"You all right?" another man asked. Then Seth got it. *Oooh, they're just greeting me. Gotta love the variety of cultures!*

Seth took a break at the next bench. It was at a viewpoint. He could see clouds in the distance over the sea. To his left, he could see some of the white cliffs. They were big! He couldn't believe he was seeing them in real life. *Far better than seeing them in a textbook.* He also noticed how green and lush the grass was. It was the type of grass you could have a picnic on or do cartwheels. One could easily spend hours sitting and reading there too. The whole scene was so picturesque. He wished he could bottle the scenery in front of him along with the exact emotions he felt. *I'd love to share this moment with Myrah.* Myrah had managed to make a little home in his mind and heart. He thought of her often - and he felt in in his gut that he would get to see her again. *Call it hope. But I just feel it in my bones!*

It was around 5pm in the afternoon and the daylight was still strong. He was keen to go further. As he walked along the path, he saw gulls darting to and fro from the cliffs. The light breeze brushed through the taller grass. Below the cliffs, he felt a sense of reverence to the wildness of sea. There was a little clearing off to the right from the path. He headed there, lay on the ground and poked his head over the cliff edge. It was incredible! Seth saw the sheer drop of about hundred and fifty metres below him. Heights invigorated him, so he didn't rush off – he just lay there taking it all in.

He followed the pathway for another half hour then decided to head back, content – he'd had an amazing afternoon exploring. *When one walks, one sees a lot more of one's surroundings.* As he headed back on to the main road of Dover, a slight drizzle greeted him. He was glad to have brought along the jacket. Seth liked the glistening of the streetlights that reflected off the wet patches on the road.

Back at the reception of his accommodation, he noticed on the menu board the special of the day: hearty beef soup. *I don't need any more persuasion.*

After dinner, he read a few more pages of Notes from a Small Island. He fell asleep wondering where the last song on the iPod would take him. He also wondered after that song how would he end up home...

37

A new day! A new adventure! He was packed and ready. He waved the receptionist goodbye, went down the stairs and stepped out of the friendly establishment onto the main street. He walked straight ahead for about ten steps and then pressed the NEXT button:

FLASH.
BRIGHT LIGHT. WHISSHH!!
PITCH DARK.
RECOVERING LIGHT.

As he opened his eyes, he was greeted by the distinct voice of the lead singer of Funeral for a Friend.
"Find in me the hope that you have never known
Find in us the faith, the faith to bring you home
I stared into oblivion and found my own"

The evidence that he was now in London was so overwhelming. Seth found himself gazing over the railing of London Bridge into the Thames. Just behind, one of those double decker London buses rushed by. He looked to his right and in the near distance those well-known red telephone booths. *I guess the colour red helps uplift the mood of the dreary weather.*
Seth stood with his mouth agape! He often did that when he was trying to take everything in. It had been a dream of his to one day see London and here he was standing on the famous London Bridge. He looked out in another direction and could see the renowned London Eye. *How could one miss it?* He saw a long queue of tourists waiting their turn on the iconic attraction.

Where to start? This city is so big! With no songs left on his iPod, he didn't have any more expectations. He did wonder how he was supposed to get back home, but in that moment, he wasn't too bothered about it. Myrah had crossed his mind. *Will I ever see her?* He knew that with the last song he could just press the REPEAT button and the song would play over and over...until the battery died. *But I wouldn't have to charge it? What for? There are no more songs to transport me.*

A tinge of excitement and concern wrestled inside him. *Oh well!* He instinctively pressed the REPEAT button and took out his earpieces. He wanted to wholeheartedly absorb the sights and sounds of London. He noticed a walkway on each side of the Thames. He saw a group of friends sitting with their legs dangling over one of the edges. They were drinking Starbucks coffee and eating sandwiches and were lost in conversation with one other. Above them Seth noticed seagulls ducking and diving. They, the locals and tourists, were enjoying the brief visit of summer.

38

In his notebook he decided to write a list of the places he would like to see:

St Paul's Cathedral

Westminster Abbey

Big Ben

Natural History Museum

Hyde Park

Leicester Square

Piccadilly Circus

And use public transport: underground trains and one of those double decker buses

As he jotted down these things, he wondered again how long the mysterious adventure would allow him in this old city. *There are no songs left on the iPod. What happens now? After London?* He decided to ignore those thoughts and head for Big Ben. *Less thinking, more living.* It was the closest attraction from where he was. He left his camera in his backpack, knowing that the images weirdly didn't stay on his camera roll. He had no photographic evidence of this trip, but he didn't let that bother him anymore. It had all felt so surreal, but it was all very much real – seeing his friend, seeing his dad, and meeting Myrah. She wasn't a figment of his imagination! *You can't make up someone like her.*

As Seth headed towards the famous clock, he walked past a demonstration of some sorts. The people were protesting for cheaper public transport. There was a TV crew filming the commotion. Seth decided to step into the shot of the cameraman and wave. *Maybe I'll be famous!* He smiled at his own silly idea.

39 (Myrah)

Myrah wasn't feeling well that day so she had stayed at home. Daytime television was the worst. Nothing on. But she just couldn't read another page. She had just devoured 138 pages. She needed a break. While eating her sandwich she channel hopped. She stopped at the BBC news channel. *What are those Brits up to?*

"Eeek!" she jumped from the couch in amazement. "Was that Seth?"

She was breathing rapidly. Had she just seen Seth wave at the camera? She was so certain. She left that channel on, turned up the volume, and went to make herself some tea. She'd wait for the next rerun of that news bulletin and make sure it was him. She couldn't help but smile, she knew she

71

wasn't crazy, and she knew she would see him again. She had no idea how - and yet there he was. In that moment she wished she could teleport to London to go and see him. But even if that were possible, she didn't know how much longer the song he was listening to would last. She would perhaps land there and he would be on to the next adventure already. A sadness filled her heart and she poured the hot water into her cup. *Should I just let him go? How will I ever see him again? We never spoke about where we lived.*

She was right! The bulletin came around and it was Seth - she felt giddy again. She pushed aside her sadness. She had to have hope, she just had to!

40 (Mystery Man)

The Mystery Man had also been watching BBC. He saw Seth too. He'd need to act soon. He was excited. His plan would work. He had written down the three consecutive numbers. *Seth will surely answer at least one of them.*

41 (Seth)

Westminster Abbey was his next stop. He decided that he would take the Underground there, so he looked for a nearby Tube station. He saw a man wearing a suit walking towards him. He seemed to be on his way to work. *Why else would someone wear a suit in London?* "Excuse me, sir, where is the nearest tube station?"

"Good day, mate." and he kindly pointed out where Liverpool Station was. He suggested to Seth that he should grab himself a tube station map when he got there. Seth nodded in agreement, thanking him as their ways parted. It was in that moment that Seth thought of a song he knew by Dave Matthews Band called Ants Marching:

"All these cars and upon the sidewalk, people in every direction – no words exchanged no time to exchange...and all the little ants are marching..."

The lyrics seemed so fitting there in that city – a city that doesn't sleep. The streets were always filled with tourists and locals (either shopping or commuting) and (if it were the weekend) there would no doubt be football fans walking to one of the London stadiums. In any stretch you could come across many accents and nationalities. Polish, Middle Eastern, Australian, South African, English, Chinese and of course those loud Americans.

I wonder how many photos are taken in any day in London.

Seth got to Liverpool Street station and made his way down the escalators to the westbound platform. He had worked out from the tube map that he had to take the Circle Line. (*The yellow line as most tourists would say.*) His stop, Westminster, was nine stops away. He had heard that the Underground could get really crowded in the early mornings and early evenings, and one could find themselves under the shelter of someone's smelly armpit. *I'm so glad the Tube is quieter during the day.*

He took a seat and noticed three things. People were awfully quiet on the train. Like there was this unwritten code that you're not allowed to speak to people. Secondly, Seth also saw that most people had earpieces in. *Oh, I must check how much battery power I have left.* There was a third of the battery power remaining. He wondered what each person was listening to. It could be anything from a motivational TED talk to hip hop or rock music or perhaps a sermon podcast. *The diversity of it all is so amazing! Different strokes for different folks!* And the third thing he noticed was that many people had their noses buried in a book. He took a mental note of some of the titles:

Mockingjay by Susanne Collins
Inferno by Dan Brown
Just Kids by Patti Smith
The Book Thief by Markus Zusak

There was also a teenager reading one of the *Harry Potter* books and across from her was an Asian tourist reading some tourist guide to London. He also saw a young man sporting an Arsenal shirt, who also held a book with the Emirates Stadium on the cover – it probably had some information and interesting facts about the team and their stadium.

42

"The next stop is St James Park. Please alight here for Westminster Abbey." The train announcer pulled Seth away from his thoughts. He grabbed his bag, stood up and waited by the train doors.

As Seth surfaced and exited the station, he felt the fresh air greet him. *It's rather stuffy down there.*

He saw the tourist signs showing the way to the abbey and headed towards it. Seth had once read about a famous plaque there that cited: *"The chief end of man is to glorify God and enjoy Him forever."* There was something about that line that resonated in his soul. And now he was on his way to the place where the saying originated.

When he arrived, it felt as if he had missed a breath - Westminster Abbey literally took his breath away! He composed himself and said a silent prayer of appreciation and respect. The two main spires towered high piercing the blue sky. The left one displayed a clock. He was engulfed by the sense of majestic respect that the building carried.

It's been said that the old churches in England and in the rest of Europe were created in such a prominent way - large spires and steeples and windows to make a statement. A statement of faith and worship to God. *Sadly, it seems that statement has been forgotten in many ways.*

There was a hustle and bustle to the outside world that surrounded the abbey. Tourists, commuters, workers, and scholars all heading in their various directions. But as Seth stepped inside the building, he was greeted with a sacred silence. He just sat for a long while. *Some things are just so difficult to put into words.*

After some time in the Abbey he headed to Leicester Square. He would get something to eat in that world-renown square. Seth craved a beer too. He spotted Waxy O' Connor's and headed in. The incredible thing about this pub is the remarkable tree that's inside. Seth read about how it was planted and lived for 250 years somewhere in Ireland, then they moved it there to the pub in 1995 - adding to the ambience. *I wonder how many conversations that tree has listened in on,* Seth thought. With his hunger and thirst satisfied, he wondered where to go next.

One could spend an entire two weeks in this massive city and still not see everything. Seth sensed he had to choose what attractions he would get to see that day and which he would put off for another time. *And hopefully that time will be with Myrah.* He mused. If there was anything these last few days had reminded him: *Anything is possible. And some things are just magical. Go with it!*

Seth settled on: catching a London bus to Hyde Park to catch the sound check of any band that may be there. He was certain he had seen a poster earlier advertising Foo Fighters. *That would be epic!* He opened his notebook and crossed off the things he had done and would be doing that day:

~~St Paul's Cathedral~~
~~Westminster Abbey~~

~~Big Ben~~
Natural History Museum
Hyde Park
~~Leicester Square~~
Piccadilly Circus

It didn't take him to long to find a bus stop with buses
going in the direction of Hyde Park. Even if he had to walk
some blocks, he didn't mind. He felt a surge of
unexplainable joy. *WOOHOO! I am alive and this is
happening!* An elderly lady standing beside him looked at
him curiously. So, he raised his right hand: "Up top!"
She winked and obliged, returning the high five. "Odd
young man!"

Seth was lucky to find a seat on the top deck right in the
front. As the bus headed along the various London streets,
he looked out of the large window:
He saw how all the blocks of flats seemed to stand
huddled closely together - they were either two or three
storeys high. The hanging baskets from the balconies, the
array of colours welcoming the sunlight. He saw how
people's homes opened right on to the pavement - it was
like the city structure and the people were intricately
connected.
He thoughts drifted wondering if he would see Myrah
again? *Does she think of me? Or has she moved on?* The
next stop snapped him back to reality. He could see and feel
the greenery of Hyde Park luring him in - almost there. *I
can imagine these green spaces in a huge city like this are
needed - to keep one sane.*

"Can you hear me? Hear me screaming. Breaking the
muted skies." Dave screamed into microphone.

"Yes, yes, I can." Seth spoke out loud. He had entered the park and could hear the sound check taking place. *Dave 'freaken' Grohl is in the same park as me!*

43

Seth felt content.

He decided he'd keep moving and walk towards Piccadilly Circus. *I wonder how many times I have seen those many advertising screens in the movies. Now I will get to see them in real life.*

Seth had walked a lot of miles already, taking in the mixture of history and modernism in that diverse city. He saw a road lined with apartments on one side and some shops on the other. He also noticed that scattered on the right side were those notorious red telephone booths of London - he could see four of them evenly spaced apart.

44 (The Mystery Man)

He was lucky because he had to rely on the 'assumed direction' that Seth would go. *With Seth being in London for the first time, the list of things he'd want to see was rather obvious.* So, when he had spotted him near Big Ben on the news broadcast, tracking out his "potential" stops was a 'calculated risk' that had worked out perfectly. He stood out of sight on the other side of the road. Hiding in a launderette. He waited, ready to execute his plan.

45 (Myrah)

In the quiet of her favourite coffee shop, Myrah found herself doodling one of those red telephone booths known to be scattered all around London. She thought of Seth.

46 (Seth)

Seth was approaching the first red phone booth. He heard it ring. *That's strange. Must be a misdialled number.* Ignoring it, he walked on.

47 (The Mystery Man)

Darn! He didn't take the bait! However, he had suspected that Seth would ignore the first call. He dialled the second number. This time Seth's reaction was more expected. He saw him pause and consider the scenario. He could see the mixture of curiosity and confusion splashed on Seth's face. *Go inside the booth and pick up the phone.* The mystery man silently wished. Seth did.

48 (Seth)

Seth had decided he'd just dive into the moment and answer the random ringing phone.

"Hello, welcome to London." He thought that would be an appropriate answer.

Holding the phone closely to his ear, he looked left and right, as if he were in some action movie.

But he didn't look behind.

"Sorry, this is going to hurt." *I've heard that voice before. Is that coming from the phone or behind me?*

He didn't have enough time to react because almost immediately he sensed the looming shadow behind him, but there was nothing he could do.

DIZZINESS.
PITCH DARK.

The last thing he remembered as he went down in what seemed to be a sleeper hold was thinking: *Can this be happening? I'm being mugged in London, on my first visit. What luck!*

As he lay there unconscious, he had the most vivid dream:

He was cycling down what seemed to be a country lane. On either side of him the lush green grass filled the meadow. It was so picturesque. He was headed toward a church. The wooden exterior was basking in the sunlight. As he pedalled, Seth heard the birds (he couldn't identify them) singing in unison to the squeak of the bicycle chain. He propped his bike against the rail of the pavement in the front of the church. He headed to the churchyard to where some tombstones peeked out of the ground. The sunshine and shadows seemed to do a sort of *tango* among the graves. He walked inside the building. As he entered, he could smell the polish on the pews that must have been recently applied. He saw a plaque attached to one stating a date: 1917. *I wonder what life was like back then.* There was a reverence about this old country church. He walked to the front where the lectern stood. Standing behind it, he looked out to an imaginary congregation – he wondered what words he would offer to them. In his mind's eye he could see 'the people' were desperate for some inspiration.

It was then that he glanced to his left. A magnificent stained-glass window stood proud on the east wall. It displayed Jesus as a carpenter. He was chiselling away at a table. It was the main scene. That was bordered by four other scenarios: Jesus with the woman at the well / Jesus with a child / Jesus and his disciples / Jesus standing on the boat, one window contained a lot of messages.

He mused at how one could probably look at the same window on various days and get different life lessons from it. A lot of effort had been put into constructing the stained glass. It seemed every colour of the rainbow and more could be seen in it. He looked down from the wall to the hue of light displayed on the ground. It was magical! The sun shone through the different coloured glass and displayed a kaleidoscope of colours on the ground. Again, Seth looked out at his imaginary congregation and spoke out loud: "the world needs more stained-glass windows."

49 (Seth)

He awoke to the sound of knocking and laughing – there he was lying on the floor of the phone booth, feeling a bit queasy, and two guys were knocking on the glass.

"Alright mate?" one of the strangers jeered at him.

"A bit too much to drink, ay?" another said pointing to the bottle next to him. It was an empty bottle of Fosters. Seth managed get out a groggy: "Yeah, thanks guys, I'm okay."

They moved on. He sat up slowly and notice something inside the bottle.

50 (The Mystery Man)

He was glad his plan had worked - they would be reunited. Seth's appreciation and outlook had moved him – *an unexpected twist in the tale.*

Both notes had been delivered, his work was done. The mystery man walked on for a bit and stepped into the next pub with a feeling of satisfaction. He ordered a pint and some bangers and mash - it was a moment to celebrate. A song by The Script played:

"Going back to the corner where I first saw you. Gonna camp in my sleeping bag, I'm not gonna move. Got some words on cardboard."

It seemed the perfect soundtrack for his accomplishment. In his life, right then, all seemed right with the world. He took a sip from the tall pint glass. He opened his laptop and reread the email that he had sent to her.

51 (Myrah)

Myrah was excited for the spontaneous team building weekend with her work. She had heard that their destination was the foothills of the Drakensburg. One of the clients that her company dealt with had quite suddenly (*apparently a sporadic thing that they do*) "spoilt them" with a weekend away.

The company was a creative P.A company: Flyby Fusion. Four other colleagues and Myrah - they were an efficient and effective team. They had earned quite a good reputation - so being treated to a weekend away by one of their newer clients, MM Music Distributors – was not an unlikely possibility. With much excitement, the team had planned to shut the office at 12pm on Friday and travel down in two cars.

To leave the tall buildings for the *tall* mountains was going to be a welcome break.

52 (The Mystery Man)

He had read that the manager from Flyby Fusion and her team had gratefully accepted his weekend away offer and that they were closing the office earlier that coming Friday.

53 (Seth)

He read the note for the third time:

Seth,

I have enjoyed how you have appreciated the adventure. I hope that through it all, you have been reminded that music is powerful - that it can transport you. And that music can even bring people together. I believe you met someone special. And I believe you would like to see her again. And I have it on good authority that she feels the same way too.

Charge the iPod - the next song should only be played on Friday. And you will noticed I have replaced your backpack with a larger one including a parachute.

Mystery Man

PS. There is a second note in your top pocket. Read it only after <u>ALL</u> songs are finished.

Seth was full of questions: *Why would I need a parachute? And why is ALL underlined and in caps lock? He must have added another song while I was out.* Seth couldn't contain his excitement. *Will I really get to see her again?* He felt for the second note, securely tucked in his top pocket.

Being Thursday, he had only a few hours left in London - he'd get to see one or two more things on his list, then get Myrah a souvenir and buy himself a new shirt for their reunion.

54 (Myrah)

That Friday morning raced by.

12pm. Office closed.

As navigator, Myrah punched in the address into the Garmin: 'Rest Easy, Winterton'

When they arrived, the first thing that she spotted was the large dam in front of their cottage. It was beautiful! There was a tranquillity about it. She saw that there was a rowing boat docked to a small wooden jetty to the left of the dam. She knew that would be one of the first things she'd be doing: getting into that boat with her book, taking some snacks and then paddling to the middle of the dam and just resting in the afternoon sunshine. *Bliss!* She smiled at the idea. After the cars were unpacked, they were given some much-desired free time.

The sun still hung high in the sky. *One of the good things of summer are the longer days.* Myrah thought about the rest of her colleagues - all five of them enjoyed each other's company, they worked very effectively together. They had just endured a few busy weeks - they had been productive and successful - and this weekend away had *fallen* into their lives at just the right time. She knew that later that evening they'd all be around a fire, sipping on red merlot and engaging in the delight of random banter. *Sometimes surface chit chat is more than enough*! She smiled at the thought. *But that is later!*

Back to the present, the whole team ventured off in different directions: Jane headed to a quiet bench at the south side of the property, from there she'd be able to see the splendour of the Drakensburg Mountains. She took a book with her.

Their team leader (aka the boss), Mary, poured herself some white wine and sat at the table on the terrace. Just her and the filled glass, soaking in the stress-free moment.

Alvin, the tech guy, took his iPad and went and sat under a nearby tree. (They all knew he had loads of geeky games on there.) That would keep him entertained for hours.

Marty went for a nap.

Myrah, stocked with two muffins, a camera and her book entitled "The Hundred-Year-Old Man Who Climbed out the Window and Disappeared" headed towards the jetty.

55

As she climbed into the little rowing boat, some random lyrics popped into her head:

"Won't you stay for awhile... it's been too long since I've smiled..."

She couldn't place them at all. But they were heart-warming lyrics, making her think of Seth. *If only he were here.* It had been a few weeks since that wonderful night in the wilderness, but the memories of him were still so vivid: his voice, the way he spoke, the sound of his laugh and his smell.

She rowed out to the middle of the lake and put the oars up. She noted how the sunlight glittered on the water like little diamonds dancing. She decided to lay on her back in the boat and she looked up… *Is that someone with a parachute up there?*

56 (Seth)

Goodbye London. Thanks for an incredible day! Seth read the name of the band and song on the iPod: Twin Forks – Crossed My Mind. *Never heard of them. Good band name.* He was ready! He pressed PLAY.

FLASH.
BRIGHT LIGHT. WHISSHH!!
PITCH DARK.
RECOVERING LIGHT.

"From time to time, you cross my mind. Good company is hard to find."

As he opened his eyes - he freaked out! He was falling... out of the sky! *This is why I needed the parachute!!*
"OH, MY WORD! AAAGH!" but the air rushing past him swallowed his feeble screams. Out of all "landings" this was the scariest but also the most adventurous - and he hadn't even 'landed' yet, literally. It all happened so quickly and Seth took it all in so naturally - his fear replaced with a natural skill of skydiving. *This adventure has allowed me to discover hidden talents.* He was confident of what cord to pull to release the parachute that he was wearing, so he decided he take in the breath-taking scenery for another thirty seconds or so and then tug hard.
It's funny how thirty seconds of free falling feels like an eternity.
Seth saw some of the Drakensberg escarpment to his right. From up there, he felt as if he "towered" over those

huge mountains that from the ground would usually loom over any person. He raced by some thin stratus clouds. The thirty seconds was up! He yanked the chord - the opening of the parachute jerked him upwards briefly and the resistance of the open material slowed his fall drastically. He had about four hundred metres left to go so he drifted downwards in a circular motion. It was then he scouted for where he could land. He noticed a lake to his left and saw that some girl was lying in a boat. She looked pretty content and from up there he could see that she looked pretty too. He then saw an open field besides the lake. *I can land there.*

(He had subconsciously restarted the song that had played through his ears. Although up there he could not hear a single word - the rushing air was his present soundtrack.)

57 (Myrah)

She saw the bright colours of the parachute - it was mostly a striking yellow with stripes of red and green that ran vertically down the material. She saw how the parachutist was coming into land so gracefully. He looked so free in those circular motions. *Looks like he will be landing nearby.*

She sat up and looked at the nearby open field. He was then just a few metres above the ground. She thought it might be rude to stare, so she opened her book and tried reading. *It's amazing how a book can transport one to another place. I'm in a boat in the Drakensburg now but I'm also with this hundred-year-old man somewhere in Europe.* She felt content and rested.

But also, a little inquisitive about the jumper.

58 (Seth)

He had no idea what to do with the massive parachute. After unclipping himself from it, he tried as best as he could to fold it up. There was no manual for his adventure, so he had to just wing it a bit. He decided to hoist the parachute onto his shoulders and carry it to the edge of the field. *Perhaps the girl in the boat or someone else would have need of a parachute.*

He was humoured by the prospect: a random stranger approaching other strangers with the offer of a parachute. *Odd indeed!*

59 (Myrah)

Myrah saw him lugging the big parachute. *Perhaps he needs a hand.* She rowed back to shore.

60 (Seth)

As he walked on, he saw her rowing towards the shore. Suddenly, Seth stopped. His heart was beating faster. He dropped the parachute to the ground. He saw a red tint to her hair that illuminated in the sunshine. But it was those shoulders that were so recognisable. It was her. *This is happening!*

He ran. When he got to the fence, he jumped right over it and continued towards her shouting her name.

61 (Seth)

"Myrah... Myrah." The guy was running towards her. *Is he shouting my name?* He was about a hundred metres away now. Then, she recognised him. *This is happening!* She leaped out of the boat - she was only a metre or so from shore. Her legs splashed in the 'water. And she ran.

She wasn't a good runner, but she didn't care. She pushed on. Her heart pumping. The distance between them radically smaller. "Seth... I can't believe it." He was beaming. She couldn't stop smiling and laughing.

By now the commotion had attracted the attention of her colleagues. Myrah and Seth had an audience. It all happened so fast and yet to the two of them it felt as if they were in slow motion.

62 (Seth and Myrah)

He held her in his arms. They were whispering *"hi"* to one another. They couldn't stop laughing and tears trickled down their faces.

"I missed you." He ran his fingers through her hair. "I like your hair. The red looks stunning in the sunlight." She blushed.

"I continued hoping that I'd see you again..." she started, "I just knew it, I just felt it." She tightened her embrace. They had thousands of words between them, but in that moment, all of them were left unspoken.

After their reunion they carried the parachute together to Myrah's chalet. He discarded the iPod there. He would work out what to do with it later. *There are no more songs. I don't know how I am getting home. But who cares? Right now, I am here with Myrah.*

Myrah introduced Seth to her work team. Mary opened a bottle of merlot and winked at him, "Seth, I think you have a story to tell? How do you and Myrah know each other? And how did you end up here, where we are? Have you been spying on us?"

Seth was in a bit of a Catch 22. How much information could he disclose - the whole adventure he had stumbled upon would sound quite absurd to anyone who could not think 'outside the box'.

He sipped on his wine. There was this obvious deeper connection between him and Myrah and as if she read his non-verbal cues she chimed in, "It was under an African sky, we were at a game viewing hide..." she winked at him. And he continued, "...and I unconsciously grabbed the flask of coffee next to me, which was actually hers..." they laughed.

He retold the story of their magical night. He didn't mention the iPod or how he suddenly disappeared (transported) from Myrah's life. But after the second glass, everyone felt mellow and were not bothered by all the details.

Around ten o'clock that evening, Myrah and Seth managed to escape the crowd and went to sit under the stars. A guy and a girl and the night-time sky. *Again, under an African sky.*

63

They sat there for hours catching up: laughing, crying, and sharing the days that had passed between them. The stars twinkled as if alive and as if they were listening in on their conversation. It seemed the night-time sky was drawing closer to them.

She let him share first. He went on to tell her about Sorrento, swimming in the Mediterranean and then being in Berlin and meeting up with his friend for a burger and a pint. He excitingly shared his friend's idea of them sharing the earpieces. Myrah was confident too that idea could work:

"We must definitely try that."

"Yes, we could," Seth agreed,

"But - there sounds like a but coming?"

"I was listening to the last song when I parachuted in."

She paused. "Let me check, the iPod. I think I know where the last song is..."

Seth looked at her puzzled. But he got up quickly and darted off to fetch the iPod.

She took it from him and checked out her theory.

"The last song is still on there. Did you notice that it's eighteen minutes long?"

He smiled. "There must be a secret song near the end!"

"Exactly!"

Seth continued, "However, the night is still but young, let's be fully here, before we move on."

He went on and mentioned Scotland, Dover and finally London. He shared that his "to do in London" list wasn't completed. She smiled and said, "next time, we will be doing that together."

He squeezed her hand. He thought to himself. *This feels right. This feels good.* He ended with how he was put in a sleeper hold in one of those phone booths.

"Now, tell me, what you have been up to? How many days or weeks have passed since? I seriously have no idea or way of working it out..." he paused. "My life has become filled with moments rather than days."

That's rather profound. Myrah thought. She started with the backpack she had bought. Then, her European list (of places the she wanted to see). She spoke about the Dan Brown book she had read and how she would love to see the places in Florence and the other Italian cities he referred to. She shared how she sang out loud with Taking Back Sunday.

She relived the excitement of how she saw Seth on BBC news. Seth blushed. She spoke of the chalkboard she had mounted at home with her bucket list jotted on it.
"Name any two things on your list." he asked.
"Seeing the Sistine Chapel and Oxford."
Myrah then shared her knowledge about how the Inklings (CS Lewis, JRR Tolkien and many other writers) would meet at the Eagle and Child in Oxford and exchanged writing ideas. Myrah continued and spoke about how she had begun to *value* each cup of coffee she'd had. She went on about how she would pause and appreciate each moment. She told of how she treasured the people around her: the colleagues and the strangers. She concluded with how she started being kinder to herself.

Seth loved how she spoke about ordinary things in such a profound way.

64

There was anticipation between them. They wanted to try out the suggestion from Clayton. They wanted to go on the next adventure together. But they didn't rush their time together either.
Time seemed to fly by as they sipped on wine and continued sharing stories. At one point they lay in silence,

gazing up at the stars. But they didn't dare fall asleep. They didn't want to miss a thing.

3:30am.

The others had long gone to bed. Then as if they were reading each other's thoughts they both said out loud: "Let's try this." They made their plans: loading Seth's bag with more snacks, a book for Myrah to read, her bucket list and a notebook. She also packed some spare clothes. Then she wrote a note to her team:

Hi all,
Something came up. Had to get going suddenly. No time to explain. All is good though. Will tell you all when I get back.
Bon Voyage!
Myrah

65

They forwarded through the silence after the Twin Forks song till they heard the hidden song begin. It was an old classic. They sat together, side by side. He put one earpiece in his right ear, and she put the other in her left ear. He smiled at her and she winked back and took his hand. With the backpack on, Seth took a deep breath and pressed PLAY.

FLASH.
BRIGHT LIGHT. WHISSHH!!
PITCH DARK.
RECOVERING LIGHT.

He opened his eyes quickly! She was there! *Yes!*

She looked a little dazed though - he had forgotten to warn her about the blinding light and vicious sound. He hugged her in apology and said: "Yes, it worked."

She was still a bit shaky and you could see that she was still so surprised!

"Take your protein pills and put your helmet on" were the current lyrics that welcomed them.

He took the one earpiece from her and let it dangle beside him. That was the last song. He'd be sure to repeat the song until the battery died. *Then we can work out what comes next?* Just then he remembered the second note – he needed to read that one, but first he wanted to work out where they were.

"I wonder where we are."

Myrah looked around for any clues. They were near a gate. A lot of leaves covered the floor and one could not see any soil or grass. Trees of autumn loomed over them too. The air was cool but pleasant.

"Where does the gate lead to?"

The gate was fastened to an old stone wall and about two metres along the wall, the hedge was creeping over it - it seemed the wall was being hidden by the foliage.

"Let's go inside." Myrah suggested.

Seth stepped forwarded toward the gate. There was no lock. It was just latched and there were no signs that did not permit entry. He unlatched it and pushed it slowly forward - the gate sliced through the leaves.

Myrah breathed in, "I can't believe this is happening! I'm somewhere else in the world."

They followed the path for a few metres and then came to a clearing filled with graves, but there wasn't any uncomfortable eeriness about it - but rather a serenity. Seth felt a sense of mystery too. They decided to walk among the graves reading some of the headstones. There were probably only sixty graves there. Then Myrah saw it and she gave a little gasp.

Seth asked, "What is it?"

She beamed back at him. "It's CS Lewis's grave. We must be in Oxford."

Seth smiled at her. "And Oxford is one of the places on your list. This is so exciting. We have a lot to explore here."

CS Lewis's books had been such an encouragement to both of them in their younger years. It was a sentimental moment standing there by his grave. They could feel the weight of it. They both sat on the ground. Seth ruffled the leaves that lay beside him. The foliage and wind also seemed to pay homage to the gravity of the moment.

They left the graveyard and headed into the hustle and bustle of Oxford. As they walked in to the busyness of the city they felt connected to the people passing by, some were students who were rushing off to class and the others were lingering tourists, who gazed up at the steeples and gargoyles. The past and present seemed to dwell hand and hand.

It was all so charming, seeing the cobblestone roads, the old stone walls and buildings, and you couldn't miss the beer kegs waiting outside the pubs.

"Oh yes, I have another note to read." Seth blurted out almost startling Myrah.

"Did that thought just pop into your head?" she teased.

"Yes, basically! Let's find a bench. We can read it together."

"Over there," Myrah pointed to one a few paces away from a coffee vendor. On the way past they got some coffee. They felt like locals.

Dear Seth and Myrah,

I am so glad you have finally been reunited. An unexpected twist, even in the plot I had planned. But I am most grateful for it. Your story has moved me.

So, there are no more surprises. Well, at least, no more surprises for you both, from me.

Life is a gift and it's a journey. There will be surprises along the way, hopefully most of them will be good. But even when the unexpected difficult ones come, learn from them too - always grow in appreciation and in wonder too. There are no more songs on the iPod. No more hidden tracks.

From now on, you "write" your own story. You add the soundtrack to your lives together.

I have other plans for that iPod and for the next person who will receive it. Please follow my instructions carefully:

1) Please charge the iPod fully.

2) Then I want you to each add five songs, the genre and age of song doesn't matter. But please give this some thought. (However, you only have 24 hours after reading this.)

3) Then, once the iPod has been reloaded, I want you to find Once Upon a Time. Go and sell it to owner. You will get a decent amount for that iPod because it's a rare model.

4) Use that money to book two train tickets for you two to go to France, I believe the Notre Dame should be your next destination. And then from there - you're on your own.

5) Make your own way back home, wherever you decide that is.

Thank you for letting the music transport you.

From the Mystery Man and "MM Music Distributors" (By now Myrah, I hope you have worked out what the MM stands for.)

They decided they would drop the iPod off the next day. But before that, Seth wanted to give something to Myrah. He said to her:

"Before we carry on, take a look at this."

"Hmm, what is it?"

He opened his backpack and pulled out all the letters he had written to her. He kissed her on the cheek and said, "I will give you some time. I will go get us some more coffee."

He walked off and after a few steps, he looked back at her. There sat a beautiful girl. With words on her lap. *Is it just me, or does there seem to be music playing from that bench?* He shook his head. *I think I have had this iPod for far too long, I'm hearing things now.* He chuckled.

66

The next day they found North Street and headed along there. They both wondered what the store would look like and who would be the next lucky owner of the iPod. The afternoon sun's beams pointed the way for them, and they noticed how the rays sliced through the shop window.

"There!" Myrah pointed.

Seth read the store name: "Once Upon A Time; what an appropriate name."

It seemed right that the iPod would end up there. That shop seemed so deserving and they noticed that the owner wore a tweed jacket. He looked the part.

"I was expecting you two."

"Really?" Myrah asked.

He chuckled. "Just kidding. But isn't that a great way to way to greet customers? So, how can I help you today?"

Seth pulled out the iPod. The man across the counter beamed and gasped at the same time.

"Wow, what a classic! How much are you selling that for?"

Seth asked him to offer a price. They agreed upon a reasonable amount.

"First thing though, we would like to leave some songs on there for the next owner. We both believe that music can…"

"…transport you" the man offered a reply. Myrah nudged Seth.

He continued. "Strangest thing, I had a dream last night. And that line appeared a few times in my dream: Music can transport you. Also, in one part of my dream, the words were graffitied on a wall.

Seth and Myrah each put their five songs on the iPod with no explanation to one another – it felt right not to explain their choices. They bid the store owner farewell and headed out. Seth turned right and Myrah followed. The river in the distance seemed like the perfect place to start. *To start what? The adventure was over?* They walked on without words. Seth felt a little bit lost for a moment. Myrah respected the space needed. She felt the warmth of the sun settle on her.

With each step towards the river, Seth replayed the last few weeks or days (his time measured in a flurry of various chapters.)

He recalled the various lyrics from the songs he had heard, the smells, the sights and even the warmth of the sun from various cities he had visited. He was thankful he had written down some memories of his experience.

"One does not learn from experience; one learns from the reflection of experience."

The experience of that mystery adventure had changed Seth. He was filled with wanderlust, perspective, gratitude and a newfound joy and peace. He glanced over at Myrah.

She is real. I have met someone. She's a keeper. He really couldn't explain it. *But do I have to?*

*

Just then as they walked, with a little gap between them, they both a felt a strange sensation. It was as if they walked through an invisible plastic sheet. They both *felt* it. Myrah and Seth felt as if they were passing through from one world to another: from the mysterious adventure back to reality.
Yes, that's what it felt like!

Right there, together in Oxford - that was their reality. They were in a new country. Life was now theirs for the making. They were much alive and well. They reached out for one another. They decided to find a local internet café and contact their families - to try explaining the last few days or weeks and to reassure their families that they were safe and now in the UK. They'd explain too that they were going to be there for a while - wanderlust had still many adventures planned for them. After some time, they headed out of the café and headed to a local restaurant for an early dinner.

Seth was grateful for the warmth in the autumn air. They chose a table outside. Their ciders were refreshing and while they waited for their food, they discussed things that they could do next, about finding a place and finding jobs and well, doing life together.

"But first things first. When are we booking those train tickets for France?"

67 (A man with the tweed jacket and a girl named
Alison)

One month later.
On North Street.

A girl opens the door of the second-hand store. A bell
overhead chimes and the store owner smiles at the prospect
of another infrequent customer. He thinks she must be in
her mid-twenties. Perhaps a student here at the university.

That girl never used to believe in miracles - but this past
week that belief changed, and it was about to be changed
even further.
"Good afternoon, lovely day, right?"
Briefly her mind drifted. Those were the words she had
heard earlier that week:

It was a Wednesday. She was at an all-time low. She
felt invisible and was hurting. She had done what she
normally did when she felt down – she walked. But that
day, her steps felt heavier. Life was weighing too heavy on
her soul. And so that day she walked in a different direction.
She walked through Aston's Eyot.
Along the way she thought she had heard music and she
tried to find where the sweet melody was coming from.
There were no churches in the near vicinity and there were
no music halls nearby.
Could it be? Is the sound coming from that bench?!

As she approached the bench, it had seemed that the music got louder. It was as if they bench was inviting her to sit and so she obliged. Then the music stopped. *Am I losing my mind?*

But there was something about sitting on that bench. It was as if peace sat alongside her, and that's why she glanced to her left where she saw something on the bench: it was a postcard. On the cover was a stunning picture of Oslo. The city lights reflecting on water of the bay.

She turned it over.

Dear Alison,
Your dream to see the Northern Lights will come true.
Will you let the music heal you?
TFK – Breathe You In
Address: Once Upon a Time. North Street

Her hands were shaking and her heart was beating so fast. *How could this random postcard be addressed to me? Is it just coincidence?* And just at that moment a guy on a bicycle (who looked so free) rode by greeting her:

"Good afternoon, lovely day, right?"

She snapped back to her present: There she was on a Saturday afternoon in a quaint store called: Once Upon A Time. Alison smiled at the store owner and replied:

"Yes, it is a glorious day!"

She saw the postcard on the counter. It was the same as the one she found on the bench. *What!*

"Was it you? Where did you get that postcard?"

The storeowner looked a bit confused. And then smiled.

"Are you Alison?"

Her eyes widened. She took two steps back, grasping her cheeks, suddenly feeling faint. *How on earth?!* He asked her to sit and then offered her a cup of tea.

They sat at one of the antique dining table sets and the words between them sprang out like a bubbling brook. She told him about how she had been feeling down and how she went out for a walk in a different direction hoping to get some answers. She then told him about the bench and the music that seemed to be coming from it. She told him about the peace she felt on the bench, the postcard and that it was addressed to her. And she shared how Oslo was on her travel bucket list and how she had hoped to see the Northern Lights one day. She spoke about how she had often felt *unseen*. But since that day of the bench and the postcard she had felt freer and part of a greater story.

She paused briefly. "The name and address of your store was on the postcard." She then blushed. "Sorry, I just spoke a lot there."

He smiled back and went on to tell her how the day before, he'd opened the store and seen the postcard on the floor. He'd picked it up. It too was addressed to him. All it said was: Give the iPod to Alison. And at the bottom was written: PS. You will be reimbursed, generously. He went on to say that there was a considerable amount in his account.

"Hold on Alison, let me get it for you."

When he returned, Alison was in tears. "Are you okay?"

She wiped her tears with her sleeves. "Yes, I forgot to tell you what else was on the postcard."

Alison told him about the song suggestion: TFK – Breathe You In.

She grabbed her phone, opened YouTube, and played it:

"Taking hold, breaking in
The pressure's on, need to circulate
Mesmerized and taken in
Moving slow, so it resonates
It's time to rest, not to sleep away
My thoughts alone, try to complicate
I'll do my best, to seek you out
And be myself, and not impersonate"

"The lyrics touched my soul in such a profound way. I had never heard of TFK before." she said after the song. "I realised then that Music is powerful, it can…"

"…transport you." He replied. She felt the goosebumps on her arms. *Wow!*

She left the store with the iPod and excitement. *I wonder what songs are on here and why this iPod was given to me?* A little way down the road, she stopped, plug in the earpieces and pressed PLAY.

FLASH.
BRIGHT LIGHT. WHISSHH!!
PITCH DARK.
RECOVERING LIGHT.

The Confessions of a Domestic Worker

To whom it may concern.

My name is Beauty. (Well, that's my English name. Apparently, my birth name is too difficult for my employer to pronounce.) So, I figured if I settled for a simple name, it would make things easier. Besides, my name is quite fitting because my life is beautiful! I have switched on Mr Avery's computer to type out my story for you:

I have two children. Ayanda, my eldest; she is in Grade 10 at Klipspringer High School. She loves dancing! Often, in the evening, I will take a sneak peek into her room and see her practising some dance moves. (I must be sneaky because she gets all shy in front of me. You know how teenagers are.)

Kagiso started high school this year. He loves soccer. One of my favourite things is to see him and my husband supporting their favourite team: Ajax Cape Town. They sit huddled together on a Saturday afternoon shouting at the TV. (I keep telling them that the players can't hear them through it. *That joke never gets old!*) They both just "shoo" me off with their cheeky smiles.

Solomon, my husband is a hard worker. I am so proud of him. For the last two years he has won Best Salesperson of the Year. He works at the local nursery called Green Fingers. He is knowledgeable with all things gardening and he is super friendly and helpful with every customer he deals with. They even return to the store asking to be served by him.

I have been working for Mr and Mrs Avery for about seven years now. I love their kids too. Megan is in Grade 6 and she loves to sing, we often sing together after school. Their son, Matthew is in Grade 8. (Kagiso and he are friends.) Matthew so desperately wants to play in the Under 14's first team with Kagiso. I think that will happen soon - I'll tell you more about that later...

I'm no ordinary "maid." Oh wait, sorry: domestic worker (to be *politically correct!*). Read on, and I think you will see why. Most of us in this industry work from 8am to 3pm, our job responsibilities include vacuuming, mopping, doing the washing & ironing, washing the dishes and other general cleaning. I work on Mondays, Wednesdays and Fridays.

I enjoy my job! My responsibilities also include fetching Megan and Matthew from school at 1pm & 2pm respectively. Oh, and I work till 4:30pm, but I don't mind the extra hours. Besides more pay, there is a lot more to my day than many realise.

I am incredibly grateful to Mrs and Mrs Avery. They have been particularly good to me and they even pay the full school fees for Ayanda. (That really does help Solomon and I a lot.) So, I return the favour to them in other ways...

Okay, okay, I will stop being all mysterious and get to the climax of my story. (On that note: I have learnt, online, 'how to present a story'... so I am trying it out with this *confession*.)

I honestly don't know how all the other domestic workers take so long to do everything - they must really dawdle! I get to the house around at 07:30, enjoy a cup of coffee, say a little prayer and then start my day at 8am. I am usually done by 11am. Maybe 11:30 max! So, I know what your next question is: "What am I doing with the rest of my day?"

The Averys have internet at home. And I didn't want to waste that free resource, so I got creative. Ayanda learnt how to connect to the Wi-Fi with a subject she does at school called CAT (Computers and Technology.) She gave me a quick crash course and now I know how to use it too. In the morning, one of the first things I do is put the SMART TV on. (It really is smart! You can browse the internet through the TV.)

I navigate to the TED talks on YouTube and while I am washing dishes and doing the ironing, I am learning some new things. *Why not?* There are a lot of interesting things out there that one can learn. And it's free! I've learned how to have better conversations and that has helped me with Mrs Avery and our own neighbours back home. I have also learned about the surprising habits of original thinkers. I shared what I learnt with both Kagiso and Ayanda. (They're going to do great things one day, I believe it. #proudmom)

I also heard an inspiring talk about how to teach girls bravery rather than perfection. Some of the knowledge there I have also shared with both Megan and Ayanda. I would be thrilled to think that when Megan one day becomes a teenager, she won't be sucked into all that unnecessary peer pressure that is so rife out there. Social media is full of nonsense! And I have seen over the years how it affects all cultures: Black, White and Indian.

I confess, I am sometimes very scared for the future of these four wonderful children I have the privilege of rearing. There is so much unfair pressure on them, and the busyness of these modern times is swallowing them whole!!

So, I am convinced of my calling. I am passionate about the mandate I have over these four young lives. Because both our boys are at the same school, I asked Mrs Avery if Kagiso could come back to their house when I fetch her kids. Thankfully, she obliged. And she doesn't know, but it has truly done Matthew the world of good. 'How', you may wonder?

When all three (Megan, Matthew and Kagiso) get home, I tell them to put their school bags down and put on some play clothes. Then I take some old wood offcuts from the garage and make soccer posts at the one end of the yard. Megan plays keeper. (She is thrilled to even just be allowed to play with the "big boys.") Then Kagiso teaches Matthew how to dribble the ball. He teaches him to shoot the ball correctly. Matthew's ball sense has grown a lot in the last two months - next week he is going to try out again for the Under 14's first team. Kagiso now believes he is ready. I agree. After half an hour of play I insist that they each go take a fifteen-minute *power nap*. Then it's homework time.

However, before that we have a critical ritual that all four of us do. The Averys have an extensive library with a wide range of books: stories for kids, teenagers and adults. We each read for fifteen minutes. At the start of the year, we all made our own bookmarks. We used some cardboard, glue and glitter that I found in the crafts drawer. I encourage the reading for two reasons: firstly, to expand our imagination. (Sadly, this video game era has destroyed that for many kids.) The second reason is to help each of us with our reading ability - Megan is now the second best in her grade.

While the kids are doing their homework, I read and learn online about how to write stories. There are lots of free online courses. (I hope to write a book one day. That's one of my own goals.) If the kids need help with their homework, I gladly assist. I am not stupid! (*Contrary, to popular belief or stereotyping*). I choose to work as a domestic. It's very rewarding in many ways!

When it's home time, Megan and Matthew always run to give me a tight squeeze which warms my heart. Mrs Avery has offered to drop Kagiso and me off at the taxi rank but the walk there is not far. Plus, I enjoy the quality time I have with my son on that walk. He and I try to spot and identify various birds. (The bird book at the Averys has been helpful.) Our list numbers seventeen different species since the start of the year.

To save money, I negotiated with the taxi driver that Kagiso can sit on my lap and I buckle him in with me. It's quite fun in that taxi. All the passengers and I sing together. (I guess you could say, it's in our culture.) Kagiso has such a powerful voice. I think when he's a bit older, I will encourage him to audition for The Voice.

To save further money and to also prevent my legs from getting old too quickly, I ask the driver to drop us off about a kilometre away from our home. Once, I met a wise old "umlungu" (white person) who told me that walking everyday will keep one healthy! On that last stretch home, I encourage Kagiso's imagination again and we try seeing interesting shapes and things in the clouds.

6pm is my favourite time of day. All four of us are together. Solomon, Ayanda, Kagiso and I all congregate in the kitchen and work as a team. Ayanda will peel and slice the potatoes. My husband will prepare the chicken. Kagiso and I prepare the vegetables. (This entails taking them from our vegetable patch, washing them and cutting them up, ready to be cooked.) Then whilst the food is on the go, we wash and dry the dishes and set the table too. Before we eat and before we say Grace, each of us has a turn to say two things we are grateful (or want to celebrate) about that day. I always want my family to be appreciative of the lives we live. There is a lot to be thankful for!

Before Solomon and I head to bed, we make some tea, stand outside and look up at the stars in silence. *Okay, I lied previously* – this part of the day is my favourite! This handsome and kind man standing next to me. Bliss! I am the luckiest lady alive. We may fall asleep with a corrugated sheet of iron over our heads, but we are happy. This little place is our haven. My children are going to make it big one day and they will become a lady and a gentleman and will not backstab anyone to be successful. Not a chance!

So, this is my world, and this is my life. I am proud of it! I'd like to believe I am a positive influence on Ayanda, Matthew, Kagiso and Megan.

By the way, it is no accident that you found this in your post box and that you are now reading this. I walk past your home every day. Again, I confess that I have sometimes heard the arguing. I have seen how disobedient your kids can be. (One can learn a lot from the after-work interaction of your family on your driveway.)

In conclusion, I'd like to end with a question for you:

I have Tuesdays and Thursdays free. Would you like me to work for you?

Yours Sincerely,

Beauty
(My cell is 072 941 8036)

PS. I did switch off Mr Avery's computer and printer.

(Written: 10 April 2017)

Two sides of a coin

"Heads or tails?"

They were deciding on who would buy the next round. He chose *heads*. The coin was launched into the air. Their side of the counter was dimly lit and Johnny Cash played overhead. The two glasses were waiting to be cleared, remnants of ice cubes barely filled their emptiness.

He caught the coin and placed in on the top of his hand.

Heads (90p)

"How was your day, honey?" she shouted from the kitchen. He slumped onto the sofa.

"It was long!"

She came in with two glasses of white wine, their usual summer afternoon choice. She sat alongside him, "Anything out of the ordinary, today?"

He chuckled. "I heard your voice in my head today." She looked at him, quizzically. "What I mean is that on my way to a meeting, with only ten minutes to get there, I noticed a lady with her son, stranded. Their car had broken down. Yes, I could have driven past, I am sure someone else would have helped them soon enough. But then I *heard* your voice." He nudged her.

"I know you'd insist that I pulled over, right there and then. So I did. They had a flat tyre - so thankfully, nothing too serious, but still - I did the Good Samaritan thing and helped them."

She was proud of her husband. She kissed him on the forehead and got up to the put the oven on. "I love you," and smiled at him. He took a sip of his wine.

Tails

In the next street down.
"Honey, I'm home."

He wheeled himself to the entrance way, "Hey dear, how was your day?"
She bent down and kissed him and they headed into the lounge. "It started off well. I was productive in the office. I then fetched Ben to take him to practice – but on the way there we got a puncture."

He squeezed her hand - a wordless prompt for her to go on.

"Today's practice was when the team would be selected for this Saturday's match - without Ben being there, his chances of making the team would have been hindered.

As I pulled over, I whispered a little prayer. *God, please help us.*
"Within in three minutes, this guy pulled over and offered to help. Accessing that we needed to change the tyre, he got out the spare and the tools from the boot and efficiently replaced the tyre.
It looked like he was off to a meeting, but he never gave the impression of being hurried or irritated by the inconvenience of our puncture. When he finished, he wished us well and thankfully, Ben made it to his practice on time."

He smiled at her, "Humanity at its best, and God answering our prayers."

That afternoon Ben had had a good practice and his performance on the field made it a sure thing of his selection for Saturday's squad. After the practice, the coach took the whole team down to the local milkshake bar.

Heads (60p)

His cough has been going on for a long time, I really should check in on him - to see how he is feeling, I know what it's like when my sons are ill.

His office is just around the corner from hers. *He will probably pop in later -I'll ask him then.*

Later that day he did walk into her office, with a request for some finances for his department.

"How are you feeling?" She asks.

He smiles. "Getting there. Thank you for asking." And then he walked off, back to his office.

Tails

He sits there stunned for a moment. *I am so glad she asked. It's nice to be seen. I know a question like that was filled with care.* Even though he is alone, he knows that there are people out there - who do care.

Heads and Tails (50p)

This pain is excruciating! It's frustrating that the doctors can't give me a correct diagnosis.

She sits there in the crowded square and the cobbled stones that lay on the floor added to the charm of that quaint little European city. The tourists out there, were darting up and down – trying to take it all in. Christmas is in the air!

She sits there with the warmth of the hot chocolate in her hands and the searing pain in her back and he is at the bar. *I should ask him more things. He's a good guy, but this pain is stealing all my attention - grr!*

He waits for his turn to order and then the barman arrives, he asks for a pint of the local ale.
Grabbing the glass, he walks back to her - her and her quietness.
He smiles across to her. *This isn't going to work.*

They have some similarities and they enjoyed the attention of each other. It was a good idea to do a trip together, but now, miles from home they each came to similar and different realisations.
Having conversation with her is like trying to draw water from a stone.
He really doesn't mind silence usually, but the silence between them feels strained and uncomfortable. *I would love to infuse some life into her.*

The day after they returned, she sent a text - saying it's not going to work.
He was relieved.

Heads (80p)

"Honey, it looks like you have seen a ghost! You're so pale. Are you okay?"
The pilot sat down. He then went on to explain to his wife how the weather "up there" was so bad and how he

had to circle around the airport four times hoping and praying the turbulence would calm down.

"I've flown many years, but that weather made it the most extreme flight that I had to deal with."

She poured him a glass of Jack Daniels.

Tails

Meanwhile in another country.

"How was your time in Istanbul?" Mary asked during their first tea break.

"It was good. But our flight back was delayed by two hours…" Jill paused briefly and went on, "Aren't those pilots used to dealing with stormy conditions?"

Mary stopped stirring. "Are you kidding me? You had the privilege of going abroad, seeing the wonders of the new city - but you have the cheek to complain about your flight being delayed." She shook her head. "First world problems."

That replied stabbed Jill in the heart, but Mary was right.

Another song by Johnny Cash played overhead.

"I like this song. *Walk the line*."

"They must be playing the whole album."

"Another one, mate?"

"Yes, are we flipping for this one?

"Nah, but can I 'll get us each, a pint of that cider."

"Great, here are the coins I have left." He counted out loud what he had, "90p, 60, 50, 80."

"That's a total of £2.80. Shucks man, we're scrapping the barrel here." He looked to the bar and called out to the barman behind the counter, "Excuse me, mate, how much is a pint of your cheapest cider?"

The barman, shook his head, tired from a long shift and forced a smile and replied "£2.80"

"Perfect. We'll have one of those."

"I guess, we're sharing then."

(Started on 21 January 2017)

The Lift Off

His flight was in a few hours. Jim sat there accompanied with a cup of coffee and a cappuccino muffin. He had endured a whirlwind of emotions and a hive of activity getting to that point. Lifting the cup, with the warmth comforting him he pondered all that had transpired to that very moment. He thought of how in the past few weeks his life had unravelled and at the same time come together piece by piece as if his life was a tapestry being skillfully created...

"It's over!" The words bounced off the walls into his heart. It didn't come as a surprise though. They had been drifting apart for weeks already. The conversation between them had dwindled just like their love had. But there was no need to point blaming fingers at anyone. They joy they had experienced together would be stored in the library of their hearts. Volumes of good times displayed there - but their chapter had now, come to an end.

His heart was elsewhere. Not with another person; but with a place. The open fields and many other things of a foreign land beckoned his return – the vivid memories of before like signal flares! "It's over!" echoed in his mind again, followed by, "book the ticket..."

But with that there was much to do. *How does one pack up their current life and start a new one?* Being a list person - he grabbed his notebook and pen and started planning his course of action:

1. Get a job
2. Renew passport
3. Sell car
4. Declutter (sell smaller items)

5. Book flight
6. Resign
7. See family and friends
8. Pack the sentimental things and send them off
9. Mourn and celebrate
10. Submit assignments (studies)
11. Eat well and exercise
12. Finish strong

He had seven weeks. *Could it be done?* He felt like he had just embarked on a real-life version of "The Amazing Race". But did he also know that he would learn valuable life lessons along the way too? Jim was going to have to juggle many balls in executing his plan. He would have to use his time wisely and be intentional in his conversations and shrewd in his spending.

People matter. He has always known that. In his heart there was a tugging to re-join and serve the local church. *Why?* They have the "hands, feet and heart" that help people in the local community. *And that's what he could set his life to.* Familiar words filled his head: "Wake o sleeper!". *Was that a calling? People could do with a wake up and a stirring.* "I could do that!" he whispered in reply. Jim got straight to action – compiling a CV, filling in application forms and sending them off – praying for the right response.

One afternoon, he cut down his book collection by half. He wanted to "travel light" in a sense. *If his life were reduced to a few boxes... what would be in them?* As he was busy sorting, 'life lesson one' appeared through a book called: *How to be here* by Rob Bell. The title immediately invited him in.

Sitting there on the floor, he stopped packing and began to read - the afternoon sun joined in. He read the first two chapters and was already inspired and challenged. *He'd need to be sincerely present.*

He journalled these two quotes:

"At any moment in the day, you can only do one thing at a time. And the more intentional you are about knowing what your 1 is, the more present you will be."

"What would it look like for you to approach tomorrow with a sense of honour and privilege, believing that you have work to do in the world, that it matters, that it's needed, that you have a path and you're working your craft?"

His early evening ritual of using grey water to water the plants on the porch continued. *Why should I stop that?* To see the white flowers and orange flowers in full bloom each day was a delight!

Life is not a list though! With the things he had to do - there was no necessary order: so, some days he could pour energy into certain things and on other days he'd wait - the demands of his current job didn't take a break.

Jim had managed to book a passport renewal date at the local foreign embassy. Then one Tuesday morning he opened his email! "Woohoo!" he exclaimed. He had landed a job with a church in a little town outside of London. He said a prayer of thanks and crossed off an item from the list:

1. ~~Get a job~~
2. Renew passport
3. Sell car
4. Declutter (sell smaller items)
5. Book flight
6. Resign
7. See family and friends
8. Pack the sentimental things and send off
9. Mourn and celebrate
10. Submit assignments (studies)

11. Eat well and exercise
12. Finish strong

Selling his car was breeze! With that money he booked his flight and paid for the shipping. Things were slowly falling into place. His *new* life seemed to be stacked in the corner in a few boxes. *It's amazing how we can live with little and be okay.*

One Wednesday morning, they sat together, each with a cup of coffee. Jim let her share where she was at.

She spoke first, "My goal is to act in local television."

"I can see you doing that." He replied. *You could see her beam as he said that.*

Four weeks went to go! The first three weeks had gone by quickly: Jim had handed in his resignation and booked a few days with his family.

Another Wednesday with another student and a vastly different location: they were on top of Table Mountain. They had just done the strenuous climb up and were sipping water and drinking in the view of the bay before them. *I'm so thankful for the variation of this life!* You could see the distant peaks and you could see the ocean glittering below. A little Rock Hyrax sprang up on some rocks nearby.

The student spoke first: "This view is stunning!"

"Isn't it just? I'm so thankful for my health and physical ability to do this."

"I'm thankful for this experience. This is a first for me!"

It was a life lesson Jim had taught his students: to live with gratitude! And he too was thankful that he had the privilege of speaking into the lives of some students. *Maybe some of the things he had said with journey with them as they parted ways.*

There, sitting on the beach – he, his nephew and niece were building sandcastles. To be part of their delight was definitely a highlight.

"Let's build it higher, Uncle Jim."

"Good idea!" and he scooped a handful of sand, placed it on top and began to shape it out again. Their little giggles were so adorable and heart-warming. *Quality time stored in his heart.*

His house was looking emptier with all the things he had sold. *It's amazing how much clutter one accumulates over time.* The moving company was scheduled for the last week to collect the items that were being shipped across.

One week to go. He had just a mattress left, some kitchen utensils, a kettle a cool box and of course, the suitcase that he'd be taking on the plane. The flurry of activity over the past few weeks could not distract him from his feelings - three nights before departure, he sat in bed thinking about her: There had been love! They had wonderful moments together. A memory appeared – of their time in Clarens:

They sat on the table outside the brewery. They had ordered handcrafted ciders with a distinct pear and apple flavour. The drink fitted the ambience of the moment together and the town they were visiting. It was an artsy and quaint town. With antique shops and art galleries scattered around the main square. That afternoon they had bought freshly baked bread from the local bakery. It was still warm as they carried it home. That evening they had found second-hand winter coats from a charity shop. What a bargain they were! He was fond of the coat. And he was fond of her too.

But it was now over! He fell asleep with loneliness and tears.

121

He woke up the next day with a scripture floating in his head: "this is the day that the Lord has made, I will rejoice and be glad in it." *Amen!* His conflicting emotions would continue the *tug-of-war* within him – but that is part of the process. But he also knew - each day was a gift! *Breathe.*

The second to last day was filled with varied conversations with colleagues and students - sharing their highlight reel of the previous months together.

There is always time for a beer. Early that evening, he headed down to his favourite local pub: The Old Bridge Tavern. He sat there taking stock of his life and mentally checking that he was ready for the next day. He pulled out the mini bookmark his brother had given him. He had stored it in his wallet. His brother knew him so well. He had written on the back of the bookmark appropriate lyrics by Pearl Jam:

"And now he's home and we're laughing, like we always did...

My same old, same old friend...

Until a quarter-to-ten...

I saw the strain creep in...

He seems distracted and I know just what is gonna happen next...

Before his first step...he is off again..."

D-day! He placed the cup back on the counter and snapped back to the present. He looked one last time at the empty house around him. Grabbing the scribbled list, he reread all the items and checked that he had everything:

Passport, laptop, camera, locked suitcase, ticket and a novel

The taxi arrived.

"It is funny how when one nears the end of a really good book, you savour the last few pages, because you don't want the story to end." The cab driver looked at Jim through the rear-view mirror. It was if he was reading his thoughts.

On the way to the airport Jim took in his surroundings for one last time. The jagged mountain peaks pierced through the crisp blue sky. The clouds had not joined in yet. The morning sunshine stroked the contours of the mountainside. *Jim never tired from seeing those mountains.* He glanced to the other side of the vehicle and saw the sea on the horizon. He had cycled along that beach's promenade countless times. *One sees the world quite differently from two wheels.*

He stood in the line waiting to check in and noticed a lady two places in front of him: she wore a blue dress and her hair hung loosely. She looked like a *free spirit*! She looked like summer! But what also caught his attention was the book she held in her left hand: "Much ado about nothing" by William Shakespeare. *Oh, how opposite my life has been to what that title suggests.*

A few minutes later, he was buckled in and the engines roared to life. He peered out the window as the Boeing made its way to the runway. Then, full throttle and they were off. As the plane lifted off, he felt a weight lift off from his shoulders. Jim smiled. *A new chapter had begun.*

The Weight of Happiness

A lot happened that week. It was as if each day had more than twenty-four hours in it. It was a Tuesday in the autumn of 2014, when that very peculiar thing happened.

My brother and I were in the town square. That's where a lot of the students met after their college classes. There was always a hive of activity. The focal point was the stunning water feature, around which was a well-kept piece of lush-looking grass, (Much respect to the town council who did the gardening there.)

After stressful classes, a bunch of us would often meet there, either to catch up or just to chill. There was a coffee shop owned and run by a quirky barista who always wore floral shirts. He'd tell his customers that he was just trying to keep the memory of Madiba alive. His cappuccinos were the best. There were benches for shoppers to sit. For the skaters, there were rails scattered around the courtyard of the town square. Red and yellow roses decorated the flowerbeds bordering the live stage area. Over the weekends there would be live performers, both musicians and poets. Groups of girls would regularly sit on the grass chatting away, taking selfies and listening to their iPods. Autumn leaves danced over the cobblestones in the light breeze. Another picturesque afternoon.

It was indeed a hip place to be.

My brother and I had planned to meet at 3:00pm at "Joe's Milkshake Bar" next to the coffee shop. We were fans of Instagram, so we were capturing some shots of the afternoon sunlight spilling down among the students. We got some good photos of the skaters and even some sparrows nibbling on the left behind crumbs. On a nearby lamppost, I noticed the poster advertising the new Taking Back Sunday album: *Happiness is*. It was on one of those thin Masonite boards. The one string that held up the sign had come undone. My brother was kneeling below it, trying to capture a ladybird on a blade of grass lounging in the sunshine.

Then...

It all happened so quickly!

I momentarily glanced at the Special's poster on a shop window, then THUD!

I saw that my brother was lying on the ground, the Masonite board lying next to him, as if not trying to conceal its guilt. I dialled Emergencies. Ten minutes later they were lifting my brother onto a stretcher. He was lights out! I saw the bump on his head - it was abnormally huge.

Happiness is. Yeah right! I thought to myself as I tossed the poster in the nearby bin.

He came around about an hour later in the local hospital, Stanford Heights. I remember sitting in that waiting room, feeling the sense of anxiety, glancing at the faces around me – portraying discomfort.

He was discharged and that's when it all began...

5:55pm.

As we walked through the waiting area of the hospital, I noticed a very strange thing.

The little restless toddler from earlier suddenly sat still - a smile arrived on his face. The baby in the blue pram stopped crying. The young couple I had seen fighting in whispered tones, held each other close, love accompanied

125

their connection. The eleven people, all waiting there seemed at peace as my brother and I walked by.

It wasn't like that earlier, I swear.

I had cycled home from the town square, fetched the car and headed straight for the hospital. I had remembered thinking how restless that waiting area had felt as I walked through to the room where my brother was recovering.

As we walked outside through the push doors, I heard the earlier commotion start up again. It was as if peace followed us to the outside world. The afternoon sun welcomed us in the car park, but I noticed that my brother looked quite downcast.

"Are you okay? Are you in pain?"

"Nah, I'm not in pain. I just feel kind of emo." he replied.

"Well, you probably just need a good sleep." I winked at him and shook my head. "Odd boy, you are."

Wednesday 7:00am.

She was at it again - my mother moaning about so many of the usual things. (She's such a worry wart.)

"The petrol price is going up again. I'm not sure if I can afford another price increase. The supervisor has been asking me lots of questions at work. Is she going to fire me?"

Blah, blah, blah. I stirred my cornflakes as if I were mixing some magical potion.

"Mom, you need to stress less." Then he walked in. And she was a different person:

"What a glorious day!" "Isn't the sunshine just so wonderful?"

What, who is this person? Who abducted my mother? I looked to my brother. *Did he just wince? I'm sure I saw his face flinch as if he was in pain?*

My mom kissed us both and headed off to work.

"How are you feeling, Oliver?"
"Pain wise, I'm all good. I don't feel any discomfort. But man, I had some seriously messed up dreams."

He went on to share them with me. They were dark. And he had dreamt a lot - like he was having the dreams (or rather, nightmares) of other people too. *His poor mind.*

Prior to the accident, we had set that morning to go and pay the TV licence at the Post Office for our mother as we only had lectures on Wednesday afternoons.

Oliver said he was still keen on coming with me - he needed to get out. He hated having 'cabin fever'.

10:15am

I knew going to the Post Office was going to be a mission. The government institutions in our country are so darn slow! As we got to the entrance, I could see the queue was already thirty people strong. *Shucks, I thought with it being the middle of the month, this place would be quiet.*

Oliver had left the actual licence paper in the car, so I offered to wait in the queue in the meantime. You could feel the despair in that place. I looked around. People wore frustration on their faces unapologetically. A middle-aged lady was speaking rather loudly on her mobile phone rebuking the poor victim on the other end. She was going on about the other person being selfish and not appreciating her.

127

Does this lady think we care about her woes? So inconsiderate!

Funny, how contagious negativity is...

The first lucky fifteen in the queue were able to sit and wait, while the rest of us stood wishing the line to shorten quicker. I saw a man with a grey beard wearing a blue shirt and some flacks. He was sitting in the fourth chair tapping his legs up and down. Clearly, he had elsewhere to be. I was worried he was going to wear his soles in with that amount of tapping.

Then Oliver came in. And it happened again. The mood of the room changed. The lady on the phone expressed her love to the person on the other side. She was smiling. The tapping man stopped. He seemed so content. The fidgeting in the room was replaced with happiness. Then I saw the anguish in his face and he was holding his stomach as if he were suffering from severe cramps.

What is happening to Ollie?

8:35pm

My brother retires to his room, his shoulders slumped. *Wow, he really has been looking emo...*

Friday 9:00am.

There was another errand we had to do. We needed to get some banking/student loan issues sorted. That morning turned out to be the worst morning ever. And *weirdly* extraordinary at the same time!

Ollie and I sat comfortably on the maroon sofas in the reception area. We were chatting about the latest football scores and headlines. The bank was moderately busy when *they* came in - six of them wearing balaclavas. They each held an AK47. - A gun you don't want to cross paths with.

Fear entered with them. A moment of panic shot through the staff and clients. The obvious ringleader shouted for us all to lie flat with our hands stretched above us. I heard the teller behind the nearby counter weeping.

These guys were efficient, and all had a particular role to play. The tellers were filling the bags with cash and no customers were offering up any resistance. Everything had been well-planned and all seemed to be running smoothly for them, except one thing - they hadn't bargained on my brother'

What is he doing?

Oliver stood up. Then it seemed like everything was in slow motion. He just looked at each one of them. There was something about his gaze. One by one they each lowered their weapon. And ignored the bags of cash. They then kneeled in surrender. The security guards on duty jumped into action and cuffed the six men. Relief, happiness and cheers filled the room as everyone stared at my brother in amazement.

Then as if he couldn't stand the weight of it all, Oliver collapsed.

I got to ride with him in the back of the ambulance. He didn't look well. There seemed to be a darkness that filled his face. As he lay there in agony, I thought of those past few days. Oliver had seemed to change the mood of each place, as if it were an ability or some superhero power. First, the hospital, then at home, thirdly, the post office and then (just then) the attempted bank robbery. Was it possible that all those negative feelings experienced by the people in each situation had accumulated into one massive emotion that my brother had to bear?

Was it Spiderman who said that said with great power comes great responsibility?

It was hardly a time to be quoting fictional characters - but it was a strange week!

My brother ended up in the room next door to the one he was in three days before. My mother and I sat in silence as he slept. (There is always an eerie feeling about the quietness in a hospital.)

Saturday 5:15am.

I had woken up with a fright. My mother had left. The comfort of the couch had called me to stay the night. The drip was still attached to him. *I wonder if he has woken up yet.* The nurse came in and did the usual tests. She said he hadn't woken yet. I was worried. The nurse professionally hid her concern.

Sunday 5:30pm.

It had been such a long weekend. Waiting there with the words on my lap - the Lee Child book open, but not even Jack Reacher could distract me from the anxiety that accompanied me.

Then she walked in. She was breathtakingly beautiful and she wore her gorgeous smile with ease. I also noticed how the darkness of the room seemed to lift as she strode towards my brother's bed.

I said hello and asked who she was.

All she did was raise her finger ordering me to be silent. I complied. Then she pulled out an iPod and docking station from her backpack. She seemed to be looking for a particular song. Then the scariest thing happened. She pulled out the plug of the machine that was monitoring my brother's heartbeat. I freaked out and jumped up towards her. She turned instantly and punched me in the gut.

I dropped to the floor, winded.

While I was regaining my breath, I noticed that she plugged in the power cable from the docking station into the now-vacant plug socket and then she pressed PLAY:

"You live your life like you're not in control,
Like you're playing a role
Flicker flicker fade,
Destroy what you create and wonder why it always ends the same"

The words filled the room. The mysterious girl walked out. I looked to the screen on the iPod. The artist was Taking Back Sunday. Then I remembered the sign that fell on Oliver.

"I had the most amazing dream!" Oliver said beside me. He was sitting up, his faced seemed aglow with happiness.

The following Tuesday 3:05pm

We were sipping on our Milo milkshakes. I looked out of the shop. There she was. That stunning mysterious girl. She winked at me. She had just hung up a sign on the lamppost. It was the same poster as the previous week:

Happiness is.

100 Words - At Dawn

The trigger shakes. Smelling smoke from the dingy club stained in my clothes. I hear the echo of those crappy techno songs bouncing in my head. Beer saturated lips. Worst of all, I feel my fear and failures - they're knocking at me relentlessly. I can't go on. Below me the waves smash the rocks. The moon hangs low. If I pull, one noise, then I'm gone. I hesitate. Then, the sun breaches the night-time sky, a vivid display of beauty. I stand, awed. I toss the gun. I am more than this. A new day arrives. I am alive!

100 Words – Community

These last few hours dragged on. Each minute packed with anticipation and delight. I am surrounded by good friends. Just hours before, with sleep in our eyes, we had wrestled the dawn, and *hit the road* with anticipation whilst the music blared from the car radio. The noise escalates as this *adopted* community grows, bound together by common interest - the reason we are here. The beer goes down well as the sun sets, our hearts are warmed. Then, we hear that crunching guitar sound, the frontman screams in the microphone, "TOUCH!" The crowd excitingly jumps! The rock show has begun!

100 words - The Platform

There stood two lives filled with memorable moments and some sadness too, waiting for the evening train. She has longed for someone to really *see* her. She's not bitter - but that longing remains. A few feet away, wrapped in his winter coat and thoughts; he too feels alone. Counting the countries, he has visited, but still he hasn't *met* her. The train halts. Stepping inside the warm carriage, looking for a seat. She got there first, however the seat opposite is empty – he sits down, she looks up and they smile - spirits lifted. "Hi there," he kindly says.

It snow story!

This past Saturday I was blessed to see (so close up) and play in snow for the first time. I felt like a 5-year-old child in a sandpit. It was awesome! I cannot really put in to words the joy I felt. I've seen snow on TV, and I've seen it in the far away distance. But standing in it! Throwing snowballs. Building a snowman. And just diving into the snow. I was overjoyed! This was a glimpse of heaven for me, and oh my, it's beautiful! Can't wait to be "home".

The funny thing, I really badly wanted my brother and girlfriend there. So, they could experience the joy with me. And it made me think; when we touched by God's grace and beauty, we shouldn't keep it to ourselves. So don't worry Warren and my girlfriend *(I took out her name)* your time will come - maybe not on this earth (not to sound negative) but when we get "home" this beauty will be in a huge abundance.

(Written on Monday 17th September 2001)

Disclaimer: Turns out that since this story was written my brother has seen snow and it's more than likely that my girlfriend from that time has too.

Trip to the Mountains

What an awesome God we serve! I was thinking as we were driving to the Drakensburg - we passed a few small villages. It was weird how each village in their own way was self-sufficient. More than that, that village was for those few residents living there. Do we, who live in bigger towns see these people as important? Do we realize that God dwells in those villages too? Are we doing our share to help those residents' experience God's love? I think so often we get caught up in the bigness of everything. Big churches, large attendance, excellent worship and maybe begin to forget about the people - *I don't know?* Just thinking out aloud.

The joy of being a passenger. Our destination was to have lunch at the hotel. But what was nice, was the "no worry" on my side. I need not worry whether the car had petrol or whether we had money to pay for the food at the hotel. I was trusting in my host.

Are you trusting in our heavenly Host: Jesus Christ? Our debts have been paid. Are we daily seeking Him asking Him for forgiveness, but more than that, just thanking him for what he has done?

"It is for freedom that Christ has set us free. Stand firm, then, and do not let yourselves be burdened again by a yoke of slavery."
Galatians 5: 1

Disclaimer: I left this as close as possible to the original – bad grammar and all.

I think why this is so special to me – is because it's a reminder and a glimpse into who I was nine years ago - someone who observes life around them.

(Written on 2 November 2011)

The Wonder of it All

Written sometime in March of 2009

I think Rob Bell said it well in one of his sermons: Everything is Spiritual, "What you look for you will find." Or in Lord of the Rings, Sam says to Frodo or vice versa: "What sort of tale have we stepped into?" (*Something like that, I think?*)

London has been different for me - not what I expected, but maybe that is what adventure is about: an unexpected turn of events.

I look around with eyes of despair sometimes (but that is not me):

"Oh God, remember you made me an optimist. I want to always look with the eyes of my heart: with love, joy, faith, hope and adventure."

2nd May 2009

I had this idea of writing this piece called: Wonder of it all, back in March and now I find myself in the warm month of May, with a new thought pattern and new scenes, and yes, it's still a journey of adventure.

As I write this now, I sit on a train - going up North West from London, a 3-hour train trip, all in all.

Where has my UK experience found me? I am on a train to Shrewsbury - I will be doing 10 days of training for work that I will being doing down on a campsite on the south eastern coast of England. There I will be a group leader / activities instructor for school groups aged between 8 and 13 years of age.

I look out this train window: Heck, I'm in the countryside now! I'm so excited. This England place is stunning in summer. It is a pretty green and the array of flowers around me is breath-taking and heart-warming. Looking out, I see green meadows with sheep and cows grazing. *Who would have thought I'd be excited to see sheep?*

I sit here thinking of how I got to this day:
I spent R18000 (a lot of money in South Africa) to get here. R6000 for my plane ticket and the rest for living and other expenditure here in the UK; and now I found myself lending some cash from friends, down to nothing. But strangely I feel free. I feel hopeful and my dependence on God is increasing.

Maybe the way this job opportunity came, feels like the hand of God moving in my life - opening doors at the right time. I feel more and more as my life goes by that God is more real than before. I know that that's an odd statement to make because He has always been real. But I guess I declare that as a faith growth within me. And this is crucial as it strengthens a foundation for my call in my life:
That is to *help others* and *share the reality of a glorious and compassionate God.* There is too much proof in my life, design, beauty and stories in the world for me to deny the existence of an incredible life changing God.

There is a great movie made recently called: Into the Wild. It's about a guy who leaves the traditional expected flow of society and decides to follow his heart and his desire to reach deep within him and discover an underlying depth to life. (*And there is a lot more to the movie, watch it!*)
However, I feel this time in the UK is for me to reach deep within. God is shaping me. As painful and scary as it

has been at times - this dying of me toward a new life in me is a journey that is so worth it indeed.

I am thinking more and more that maybe in fact I have a pastor heart: a heart for God's people. There is a lot of hurt and confusion in the world and ignorance of the way, grace and love of Jesus. And the world needs more spokespersons on His behalf.

And in this time, I'm allowing that call to grow. I listen to podcasts on a weekly basis and I just feel totally inspired and encouraged. I listen to the "sermons of the world" around me - and this deep reality of Jesus is getting stronger. *Very cool I must say!*

I am alive and I am well ☺

I write because I enjoy it a lot. It gives me some sort of clarity and in a sense - in wearing my heart on this sleeve, it may help one other out there – they too could connect with these words and know that they are not alone.

Also, maybe these words I write will inspire and encourage anyone to live from a deeper place. I am far from attaining this art of living, but each day I try and let God direct my heart and steps - and if this takes my whole life, I know clearly now that this has been worth every tear, every laugh, every moment and thought.

God is more real than real...as ridiculous as that statement is!

Hmm, this open countryside around me as I write makes me smile, I'm so happy. Adventure continues – oh, the wonder of it all!

*(**June 2020** - Coming back to read what I wrote eleven years ago is heart-warming, to see how far I've come. I*

wanted to put this in my collection of short stories as a memoir (for me) and an encouragement to you.)

Father and son
(Written 30 May 2009)

One of the maintenance guys that we work with surprised me today. He is usually quite a tough guy and like most of the English he has a loose tongue - a cussing one. Perhaps part of the macho attitude *persona*. You know, one of those typical maintenance guys. (*Yes, I guess I am stereotyping*).

Now don't misunderstand me, there is nothing wrong with the guy - he really is quite humorous and helpful.

Now, I don't know anything about his family situation, but today he had his son joining him onsite. It was simply so great to see how on this day, this man's son was "his priority, his number 1" throughout the day. All his attention was focussed on his son.

Father and son, went through many of the activities here at the centre: from driving the tractor, to KMX karting and to canoeing. It just warmed my heart to see this reunion. And the evident love.

So, I just felt like writing about it - that connection is beautiful. Jesus and His Father had that. It's incredible when dads and sons have that bond, this side of heaven. And it's awesome to know that we can (and do have) that relationship with our heavenly Father. He focuses on you. As if you were only person in His world.

However, are you willing to come and visit Him?
The invite is always there, His door is always open...

When Geography comes alive!

I am sitting in Cairo airport now. I feel in awe of this city that I just flew over and landed in. The world has spectacular places indeed. In fact, I just saw one of the Seven Wonders of the World:
I witnessed the sheer size and beauty of the pyramids.

As the morning sun rose over Egypt, I saw the dim light shine over the majestic pyramids - what a great way to start off my week and to start a Monday. I feel so blessed being able to see those pyramids even from the plane window. (Now, I have a *call* to come spend some more time here in Cairo and see the pyramids from the ground, I can only imagine how intense it must be to witness that stunning sight.)

I remember way back in school in Geography class, learning and wondering about the pyramids and the great Nile river - now I can say I have seen both with my naked eye. The Nile, wide and potent flows through the city of Cairo and through other regions of Egypt.

Woohoo, I was lucky to be sitting on the left-hand side of the airbus (plane) and was surprised with the sight of these beautiful pyramids. Wow!

(Written on 26 July 2010)

Note: I did go back in 2011 to see the pyramids. And not just from inside the airport! I even got to ride a camel. (1 June 2020)

Other small pieces

AFTERNOON WITH MY BROTHER
(Written on 1 August 2012)

On the last day of July 2012 (not that the date matters), I got to spend an afternoon with my brother. There was this idea that was introduced to the world a few years ago by an author known as Gary Chapman. He wrote of love being "shown or spoken" in 5 love languages. That idea has really resonated well with me and helped me in my dealings with others.

Yesterday my bro and I got to sit on my veranda eating a "bachelor's lunch" (Chicken burgers and fried egg on toast.) With the sun shining down on us while we just caught up with latest the happenings in one another's lives. We then headed down to Durban's North Beach to surf. (My usual attempt involving a lot of paddling against the crashing waves.)

A highlight for me was when my brother and I ended up catching the same wave. I am sure he and many others make surfing look a lot more gracious than I do. I spent most of that afternoon wrestling nature, duck-diving her waves and giving my arms a workout. I have always seen the ocean and God's "swimming pool" and the fact that I get to splash around here, I am grateful.

So, one of the love languages is: Quality Time
That to me is an important thing. I love spending time with the people I love.

I don't care about the quality of my surf or my lack of skills. (Although I do want to better myself at times); but what I DO care about is the time I get to spend with my brother.

Sitting on our boards, laughing, sharing life; indeed, that was a great afternoon.

AMSTERDAM WITH MY BROTHER
30 January – 2 February 2019

When reading through the previous moment with my brother I was filled with nostalgia and remembered a recent memory of us two hanging out.

At the end of January 2019, my brother was sent to Elst in Holland for some training for work; I organised to go meet him for the weekend there and in Amsterdam.

We both agree at what an excellent time we had together those 3 days in the Netherlands. Months later, we both often refer to that time together. That trip together was filled with such value and it will definitely remain with me (and my brother for a long time.)

If I think back, I can visibly remember the emotions that I felt on that weekend together. My brother and I have always been close; he is my best friend too. Over the years we have not had much "bro time" with just he and I. So here are some vivid memories I have of that weekend at 0 degrees surrounded by windmills and quality time. I got to my brother's accommodation before him. He was still at his training. So, after exploring the quaint town of Elst I went to the downstairs bar of the hotel. When my brother came in, we both had broad smiles. Hugged each other and ordered our first beer and then the words just poured out. Catching up on our lives, laughing and enjoying good local beer.

I have found when one is FULLY present in moments, they will often stay with you for a long time afterwards. If I look back, I can often remember the temperature, the smells, my feelings and even words spoken. (Is anyone else fascinated with the human brain? The info it can store!)

The first night after those beers we headed out into the nearby farms to look for a geocache or two. I can still hear the crunching of the snow below our feet. I can feel the tangible joy accompanying us and I remember the kiss 0 degrees air brushing our faces.

The next day we did a long cycle. I can visualise the roads we cycled upon. I can hear the words my brother spoke: "Aren't you thankful you are HERE now?" (There was more but that is between us.) I remember later during that day our hands were so cold... we could not even touch the keypad on our phones or pull up the zips or do up the buttons on our coats. We found a cosy looking place that did this incredible warm chocolate milk. That warm milk warming us from the inside and the heat of the fireplace doing the outside; made for a perfect "freeze-framed" moment.

The next evening, we were in the Alto Jazz Café in Amsterdam. I can remember that nice so clearly. Sitting in close proximity of everyone huddled in the small venue, the good beer, and the incredible music soothing our souls. As the evening came to an end, we had to cycle a fair distance in the darkness through a forest to our accommodation. It was an epic city adventure!

Of course, there are plenty of other quality moments in those 7 years between these two recorded entries. I just happened to have written these two down.

DURBAN BEACH FRONT
(Written on 1 August 2012)

I live in Durban North currently as I write this. (I am blessed to say I have lived in a few towns in the last twelve years.) I really do like the "nomadic" life at times. The last few days I have had some amazing moments of reflection and contentment along this stunning Durban Boulevard.

I go down to the beach alone, yet I feel like I am in the company of many, even though no words are shared.

I see skaters, I see cyclists, I see joggers, I see couples laughing and I see people walking their dogs.

I see community.

And this is supposed to be winter? Armed with only a hoodie (jersey/jumper) to keep me warm, I soak up the warm winter sun.

With the sand sifting through my toes and the gentle breeze blowing through my hair, I feel so alive. (You see, too many people around us just "exist" and not really live. Think about that.)

I feel content.

So often my heart and mind are led astray, by temptation.

The lust of wanting more, gathering stuff and the chasing after false beauty, and it steals a necessary virtue in me, the art of being content.

Recently, I sat on the beach, with the ocean spread out before me and I gazed at the life around me. In my heart, I simply thanked God for that moment.

I am learning to have more moments like that.

TREES – UNSELFISHNESS
(Written on 17 October 2012)

In the next suburb (Winston Park) from where I stay (Hillcrest) there is this row of trees that probably stretches on for about 5km.

The trees are spectacular. (Do not ask me what type of tree they are.)

And I can imagine them being decades old.

What is remarkable about these trees planted along each side of the road is the unselfishness they represent. My brother enlightened me to this truth a few months back. Maybe two generations ago some people decided to plant these trees, knowing that in their lifetime, they wouldn't see the full splendour of the trees that they have planted.

But they planted them anyway.

And about two generations later, we get to see and marvel over the beauty of these very tall and spectacular trees. How unselfish of those people from generations back.

Sometimes people do beautiful things for others.

Dear Child

(Written on 29th January 2000)

I saw you walking the other day
I was with you all the way
The laughter was streaming out
All your friends were about

Life for you was looking good
It was there with you I stood
It was good to see you smile
You were dancing for a while

Now things are sort of bad
The feeling on your heart is sad
Now most your friends are gone
They got something important on

When you feel abandoned, no one seems to care
I want you to know I'm still there
When you couldn't keep the pace
It was my arms that gave the embrace

And when you're feeling lonely
Remember you're my one and only
Now when the weight of sin gets you down
Remember I wore that thorny crown

Hanging on the cross I die
And you ask me why?
Cause I always loved you
And for you anything I would do

(It's unlikely that this poem on the previous page was this was the first I had ever written – but I do remember the sincere intention that I wrote this one with. I prayed it would help someone.)

Mark My words
(Ash Wednesday)
(written on 22 February 2007)

"They" like placing marks on me
Marks that tend to remain...
If I do badly, they mark me with low marks
They mark me sinner
They say I'm unworthy

And I'm seeing that "they" have marks
of their own...
Marks that they know don't what to do with
So, they point out other's marks

God, I've got many marks
Marks that make me feel unworthy...
Unwanted... unnoticed...

And this very night
The man in front places a different kind of mark on me
A mark to remember
The marks You carry
Those marks on Your wrists and ankles...

Marks that mark me forgiven
Marks that say that I am worthy
Oh God, I'm sorry I placed those marks on You...
And I hear You say back to me:
"Mark My words, child you are mine."

An Urgent Matter of the Heart

"We have a worldwide crisis on our hands" declared the Heart. "Them skin and bones are starting to panic! They're up to their neck in anxiety!"

Kindness thought to herself: *This is going to be a serious meeting if He started with that.*

"Roll call. Love?"
"Present," Love gently replied.
"Joy? Peace? Kindness?"
"Yes, we're here," I said in unison with Joy and Peace.
"What about Grace and Creativity?"
"Yep, present."

"Great! We have an urgent matter of the heart, our Heart remarked with a playful grin and wink. Pun intended."
Heart continued: "These are interesting times. The world is facing an unknown enemy. The only thing we know is what they're calling it. A virus has been unleashed."

We all stood aghast! Peace breathed over us and instantly we felt calm. Heart put a glass on the table in front of us - pouring water halfway.
"Is this glass half full or half empty?"
Joy knew the answer. "Half full. It's all about perspective!"

"Exactly! declared Heart.
A lot of good can come from this time. But let us serve the world without an ignorant optimism.
People are anxious.
People are fearful.

People will be bored."

Grace spoke next:
"We're going to see worst of people BUT also the best of people."
"Yes," the Heart continued, "And thus, we all have a crucial role to play. Regardless if Mother Nature joins us or not. We know she cannot be tamed."
Joy remarked: "She may giggle with sunshine or rain on our parade, but we will do our best!"
"We don't know how long this will go on for, but I will share my patience." Love offered.

Heart beamed. *I knew they would all be so helpful and ready.* He spoke up again: "We all know that there are two sides of a coin. And we have other enemies that could join in the battle." Kindness knew what He meant.

She spoke up:
"Thoughts and emotions are common to all people. The battle often starts within. We all know that Negativity, Sadness, Selfishness, Bitterness, Hatred will all try make a scene, grasping for unnecessary attention and stirring up dissension."
Creativity suggested:
"We need to enter as many homes as possible."
"There are certain homes we need to target first,"
Kindness said, "Ones where Boredom, Abuse and Nastiness often visit."

"I dislike those guys." Joy blurted out.
"Even the darkest situations can be turned around." Grace replied.

"We'll start with Howard Close first."

"Are you sure, it's a difficult neighbourhood?"
"Yes... but there are big influencers in those homes."

Heart continued:
"It's the whole rippled effect. One throws a stone in a pond and you see the ripples expand outwards. That's the plan!"
They all tuned into the houses on Howard Close. Heart sent them out. They were to report back in two weeks' time.

At first no one noticed Joy enter the home at number 8. The mum and dad and two boys were all doing their own thing. There was a misery that moved in the house too. One of the boys was upstairs playing with his toy cars. Little John was outside. He saw that the sun had come out and he wanted to be out there. Their garden was quite small, maybe only 3 metres by 3 metres (hardly enough for the boys to even play cricket.) The mum and dad sat on the sofa with a chasm between them. It was 4pm and dad was already on his second beer.
The mum sat there watching another episode of Dr Who. She felt crippled by dad being in the house every day - without work he said he felt purposeless. She could not think of what to suggest.
Joy looked up to the glorious sun and smiled. *Thank you, Mother Nature, for joining in.* He knew where he would start. Little John was outside. Joy sat on the floor next to little John who was just sitting there watching some ants crawling across the paving from the back door. Joy turned the little boy's attention to a blade of grass. There crawling so delicately was a ladybird. John approached it quietly, staring in wonder - it was so beautiful! Mother Nature helped again: Just then a butterfly flew in the peripheral view of John. He looked up in glee, the little yellow wings glistened in the sunlight. (Joy was thrilled that

154

Mother Nature was getting involved.) Then John noticed the birds singing too.

The boy started to giggle. It was all so wonderful! His laughter drifted into the house. Mum and dad were intrigued. Dad came to the kitchen door first to see what his son was laughing about. The brother upstairs appeared out the window above.

John was running around chasing not just one butterfly, but two. The man put down the bottle on the kitchen counter and went outside. He noticed some flowers starting to bloom on the shrub in the corner of the garden, he walked across the small lawn to scout them out. He smiled at his little boy. John smiled back, noticing now that his mum, was standing there too.

"Mum look how pretty these butterflies are! We're playing tag."

She laughed at that.

John's brother came downstairs. The Joy of the moment invited him.

The dad decided that those little flowers needed some watering. He went to get the hose. He asked his older son to please turn on the tap.

So, there they all were. Little John chasing butterflies, Mum soaking in the sun from the doorstep, John's brother joining in with the laughter and dad watering the flowers. Then the Dad had a joyous idea. He turned the water hose on the boys. They gasped then they giggled in delight! They both ganged up and chased down their dad. Dad dropped the hose pipe and it started to dance and move around like a snake. In the meantime, Mum had grabbed the bucket from the kitchen sink and filled it with water.

"Hey boys," she called. They turned their attention. *Splash!* All three of them soaked. Joy and the sunshine high-fived each other! It was a great start!

In that moment, the Dad had decided he would create a beautiful flower garden at the end of their yard. The boys decided they would learn to identify the birds and butterflies in their garden. And their Mum decided that for the lunch time meal they would all sit together, sharing a highlight from their day. And if it was sunny like that day, they would sit outside on a picnic blanket.

Peace climbed through the upstairs bedroom window of number 4. There was a lot of shouting downstairs. The Williams's marriage was in shambles! He had cheated on her and trying to rebuild that trust was tricky. Often the smallest things would turn into a row. They needed to work at their relationship.

Upstairs, Molly sat at her desk with headphones on, trying to drown out the noise. The blaring rock music did not help either, but she needed an escape. She needed some peace. *Why did Dad do such a stupid thing?* Peace placed her hands on her shoulders. Instantly, Molly felt a serenity. She took off her headphones and went to the window and looked up to the stars. She whispered a silent prayer. *If You are there, please do something?*

Just then, she noticed how the stars shimmered as if acknowledging her request. Peace squeezed her shoulders again. There, she felt it again. That calm inside.

Peace went downstairs. A silence hovered between them at the kitchen table. Hope had come through the back door. They were now both talking in a hushed tone. Hope had filled their hearts. They looked at each other. They wanted "them" to work. They were willing to put in the effort. It would take a few weeks, even months to rebuild. But they would try...

As they cradled the cup of tea in their hands and sipped quietly letting their tempers subside, they noticed how the moonlight spilled onto the kitchen floor. And it seemed that peace had come with that light.

Boredom had got to number 11 already. The single dad and his two girls had seemingly run out of ideas. Bringing up two girls on a single salary was difficult. They could not afford any of the available TV packages. And with the dad being in the DJ business, work had come to a standstill with this virus causing a lockdown on life.

Thankfully, he had some savings set aside. *How long would they last?* Mia came rushing into the dining room:

"Daddy, I'm boooorrred!" He sighed. Just then Creativity dropped an idea into his head. *Ping!* His eyes lit up. Mia noticed that. "What is it, Daddy?"

"Follow me," he said. They got up and headed to the garage.

"I need to make a hole in this plastic spade. Is that okay? I will buy you a new one in the summer."

Mia nodded her consent. Her dad cut out a circular hole from the spade. The once spade now looked like a magnifying glass without the glass part or like a spoon with a hole in it.

"What is it?"

"Let's go to the kitchen," he said, leaving her wondering.

"What are you doing Dad? What are you making?"

With a smile on his face he got out some dishwashing liquid and filled a bucket with soapy water. He then called out up the stairs, "Andrea, do you want start a party?"

Mia's older sister ran down the stairs missing every other step.

"Yeah, let's do it."

"Please get my big speakers out and put them on the driveway."

157

"The what?" Mia frowned. "What's happening?"

Andrea smiled. "I'll plug in your sound desk too. Are you gonna play Taylor Swift? Please…"

"Of course! But first a song called Bubbles by Biffy Clyro."

Creativity was now running through all three of them. Ten minutes later, Mia was outside blowing bubbles with her new bubble maker and Andrea was dancing along chasing the bubbles and singing along to the song:

"You are creating all the bubbles at night
I'm chasing round trying to pop them all the time"

Their dad did a DJ set for a whole twenty minutes. Joy filled the street. People poured out their homes and started moving their bodies too. Even the shy ones couldn't help but shake if off to Taylor Swift.

After the four songs, Mia's dad exclaimed: "Same time, next week. Hope to see you all again!" The people cheered. Boredom left the street, defeated.

The next day Mr Evans in number 12 picked up his phone. He got their landline number from a dusty notebook. (He must have got it when they first moved in.) After three rings, Mia's dad picked it up:

"Hello?"

"Hi there, it's your neighbour Mr Evans."

"Oh hello, how are you on this fine day? I hope the music yesterday was not too loud!"

"Most certainly not! That is why I am calling you. I have a Disney Plus subscription that I don't use anymore. When the missus passed, I didn't bother to cancel it. Would your daughters like it?"

When their dad told Mia and Andrea the news they were delighted!

Mr Evans felt good to have done a kind deed.

Howard Close was a changed place. The atmosphere there felt different. People were happier. Kindness and Grace filled the streets.

It was time for Peace, Joy, Kindness and the others to meet up with the Heart and share what they had been up to. First the Heart looked at Love and asked:

"How did it go at no 2?"

Love sighed and then she spoke of the strained relationship between a mother and a daughter. Maybe it was the daughter's teenage hormones. Or maybe it was the mother's heartache.

Love stirred an idea in the mother's gut to go for a walk in the nearby woods. It was a last straw! But there under the tall trees the affection and love of a lost dog started to restore the love lost between the two women. On working together to find the dog's owner, the mother and daughter *found each other* again.

The whole array of emotions had succeeded in their mission – bringing a different and positive atmosphere to one part of the neighbourhood.

They knew that their visit and work there was not a once of job. They would return, time and time again. Human beings always need to be reminded.

Heart looked at all of us with a smile, a silence filled the air - then He spoke:

"Well done all of you. Onto the next street!"

(Written in Lockdown 2020.)

Once upon a time in Tignes

A little foreword:
(September 2020) – This piece includes little journal entries and thoughts that I started compiling in my first few weeks when I was living and working in Tignes (way back in 2009/10). Some of my thoughts you can see are full of wonder and delight, and others – well, are quite ridiculous! But I wanted to add this in – after all, it is *my book* of short stories and pieces:

Once upon time in Tignes, France
Started on 27 November 2009 –

27 - 28 Nov 2009:
We met at Fleet for our trip down to Dover and then across the English Channel to France. A long trip ahead of us: 9 coaches (buses) of people. The people are pretty cool so far. *Let me be me, let me be confident.* Trying to sleep on the bus is so difficult and uncomfortable. Wow the bus driver has the coolest bed hide out type to thing to rest in. Very cool! Trying to organize breakfast was interesting. I need to learn some French phrases soon. It is scary in a good way, being very foreign. Haha. This is so surreal. An unrealized dream comes true. Being surrounded by sheer beauty. Saw an excellent view of highest mountain in Europe: Mont Blanc from Chamonix.
This is where our training will be. Paradise already!

29 Nov 2009:
Unisex bathrooms – now that's an interesting and new experience! My group that will be working in Tignes with me are awesome, a good mix of people. This is going to be a good winter season. Went to the Fu Bar – a nice

underground bar with a rodeo - Some good ol' rodeo fun! I wanted to get more sleep, but I'm actually enjoying being around the people.

30 Nov 2009:
We woke up in Narnia! There is snow all over. From our balcony rail to the street and trees below. The snow is falling constantly. It's stunning! My first day of seeing a lot of constant snow.

1 Dec 2009:
I can't even take a picture and I like my pictures. This sight is beautiful - The moonlit sky, the full moon shining on the snow-covered mountains. Wish you could see through my eyes - Wow!

2 Dec 2009: - From last night's moonlit mountains to today's sunlit ones. The backlit peaks look incredible. I can't wait to get out on the slopes next week. Training does seem a little too long. I think practice makes for better teaching. Theory is boring! A cool thing is: "whilst using the facilities" being able to look through the window at the snow-covered mountain range. (A toilet with a view!)

3 Dec 2009:
I feel a little bit disconnected today. I get in the way of me living or is it me just being quite different. I can't let the drink leak through me to be something else. *I am just not of the world. But this road is lonely. It's hard!*
The training for childcare really does suck! It's so long and overdrawn - I wish I could re-write the course material for them. The best part was on the way to Fu Bar for Singstar – us, boys went sliding down the snow on the road on our feet…foot sliding…you could call it.

I need to shine in my own way in this adventure. How to?

24 Dec 2009:

How did time get away with writing in this travel log? I guess it's a good thing I am on the slopes and not behind these keys... typing all the time. But I race through the last few days to see what comes to mind, and in no particular order:

Pigs can fly:

After being given outdated dodgy pork rations for a meal, Tom and I decided to see if pigs can fly and we each threw a huge piece of pork off our balcony. For some odd reason, that was the funniest thing!

Feeling alive and the meal that I won:

I had a day off, recently and my flatmate, James was a good ski host. He took me on some black and red runs, and I won't forget "how alive I felt" that day. Going down steep slopes and just braving it. Then we stopped for a late lunch at a pub to claim the 2 meals I won from a Facebook compo. Yes, I won something from all my time on Facebook - two damn good tasty meals!

Baby Jesus to the lake:

The job in this part of my life hasn't been the best. This week I had to look after 3-year-olds, *"and God, it's hard to bring you into my work and love them like You ask me too"*. I guess at some parts in my life, I know I am not "doing what I am called to do" but nevertheless this is all part of that journey.

Well, Tom and I took the four little girls to the lake for a walk and one of them wanted to bring along their baby doll. I told the little girl that if the baby must come, she must give her a name. She said that the baby's name is "Jesus." Now that made me smile! Actually, it made my whole Christmas week - because in this European country in many hearts, I believe God to be absent. And I am sad about that - but that child's words - was a shimmer of hope!

And as I type this song, I hear the words from 3rd Day on my iTunes singing: "His name is Jesus, Precious Jesus, the Lord Almighty, the king of my heart." **AMEN!**

Waiting for a bus:

Two nights ago, I was waiting for a bus and as I waited, I looked up at the falling snowflakes. In that moment, I felt really happy, this beauty moved my heart - another thing to remember from my travels. Grace in motion!

Life in the bowl (oh, that blue sky!):

There are days, when the sun shines in such a spectacular way bringing out the vast contrast of the white-capped mountains and the blue sky. Tignes is basically in a bowl, surrounded by three mountains - with only one entrance into the bowl. But this little secluded place from the world is stunning! Besides the astronomical prices for everyday things, the quaintness of the village can warm one's heart.

Sitting in, reading and looking after children (*which really is babysitting*):

Last Night, as I sat in the luxury guest chalet looking after the sleeping kids, I just read and drank coffee. As I sat on that couch, I felt a sense of contentment. Here I am, a "million miles away" in France - I am sitting experiencing something new. I can't really explain it - I mean I could easily read a book back in South Africa - but somehow on this winter night in France, it felt surreal and "once in a lifetime" ish!

A White Christmas:
I was alone for Christmas but somehow, I didn't mind. I felt a peace and love within. I went to Mass, a French Catholic church so the only word I knew was "Amen" and I recognized the word "Gloria" from a Christmas Carol - haha!

But as I walked to work on Jesus' Birthday it was lovely to see the snowflakes falling from the heavens and then in the evening after church I looked up and saw that the sky was clear of clouds and I saw the beautiful stars and the moon.

I felt God looking over me. And the intriguing thing I thought while in the church - is that the church building is in the centre of Tignes and the steeple can been seen all around Tignes. It's funny how the church is "kind of in the middle" of this resort - a physical representation that Jesus holds this altogether? That Jesus is at the centre of this paradise. If it were not for Him - none of these mountains and ski pistes would exist. God has provided this garden for people to play!

The Stores Guy:
It's cool having one of our roommates who works in stores. We get all this cool stuff in our flat. Food, toilet paper, etc. It may not seem that extreme but when we don't always get fed good portions it's great to have a secret supply. (Well, not a secret now - if you're reading this... haha!)

I thought that I must give you more clarity on this heading. Two weeks back, I casually suggested to the store guy that we should get some toilet paper for us. Instead of getting two packs of four rolls - he ended up bringing back

164

about twelve packs. It was just too funny! One of those "had to be there" moments.

Oops, I did it again:
I was taking pictures and a small video of a cross on a hill and when I put my camera away and tried to put on my second glove, and it fell off the drag lift. Haha! That was funny! *The number of lone gloves and ski-poles lying under those chairlifts must be quite a lot!*

Like we're in a submarine:
The mind is highly creative and incredible. My bunk mate and I laughed at how our bunk bed is rather narrow and we feel like we're in a submarine. It's a cool feeling though. I close my eyes and imagine that I am on adventure - and then I wake up knowing that I actually am on one: In France, in a small room, miles (sounds cooler than writing "kms") away from my home! I then remember those sleepless nights in my cozy home in East London where I longed to "leave that place" and experience new things! This year (2009) was not what I expected. That's a good thing! The thoughts I had of London life back in SA was very different to what I received this year. All for the better... I guess ☺

Satisfying snowboarding!
I am a "jack of all trades and a master of none." But I am not afraid to try anything. And I usually adapt my own style.
I took up snowboarding today (7 January 2010) and I seemed to catch onto it pretty easily! I am not blowing my own trumpet here (okay, maybe a little? ☺)... But it's cool

to try a new thing – and I guess I am good at adventurous things - that's a good way of putting it.

Living with others:
I have been living on my own for eight years back in SA, so to be living with people in 2009 and 2010 has been rather interesting. From having a roommate who flakes, to others who are very messy roommates - it's all been a good lesson! From a dirty toilet bowl to tons of empty bottles, lids, random paper and rubbish strewn all over our lounge / kitchenette floor… interesting times indeed!

10 Dec 2009 – This is so cool! (And transfer day shenanigans):
Those who know me well, in many ways I am an island, but I swear, living with three other guys has been pretty cool!

I am happy tonight. As we have music blaring from the PS3 and TV and we have different mates and colleagues who come by for a drink or two. *Some cheap beer or stolen chalet wine… I'm loving this new experience!*

Beer bottles and beer lids scattered on the counter and floor – and as a neat guy, this throws me out of my comfort zone, but I like it! The kitchen floor is filthy and probably unhygienic - *but what doesn't kill you, makes u stronger, right?*

This is my home! Calm in the chaos. Good vibes from music and laughter and booze and skiing/boarding.

We are so diverse but we get on. James, the guy who says odd things. 'Tommy Tignes' the all-round good guy who gets on with everyone and likes to party. Then Rich, who is our "gets a crap load of stuff for our apartment" guy and then me, the guy who writes about all these funny experiences.

I guess I am happier writing this today - because Tom and I broke the rules today by going skiing/boarding on our two-hour break. Thing is, on Sunday's (transfer day) we are not supposed to ski - company policy. But we thought, *what the heck, it's a glorious sunny day!* And we just felt so alive on the slopes.

I also look ahead to my week's Rota... what a good week ahead. So yep, I am stoked at the moment!

Two Christmas Tales
(25th January 2009)

2008 - It was Christmas Eve - the three of us were on our way home from a lovely dinner that we had with our parents. We arrived an hour late that night. The car had broken down. It was rather annoying! Why did we have to have car problems on the night before Christmas?

AD 0 - It was a long time ago in Bethlehem, their feet were covered with dust and they were struggling to keep their eyes open - it had been an incredibly long day for them. She was pregnant and almost due. He wanted to provide a comfortable bed for her. She was craving to her rest her weary and aching body in a relaxing room - but the inn was full, and all the receptionist could offer was a dirty stable. The audacity of even offering that! the night before their son's birth... **Christ**- *mas eve!*

On Christmas Day my brother and I were late for the service and as we approached the church, we saw that the car park was full and therefore had to park further away. We decided to take this footpath shortcut up to the church, it was overgrown with weeds and we had to climb through all of that and jump a wall to get to the church service. We wanted to go to that service – after all, it was Jesus' birthday and we wanted to celebrate that! We were determined to get there - to see and remember Jesus...

The shepherds heard about Jesus from some angels. They went to explore and see Jesus. Nothing would stop them. Jesus the King of the World had been born, why would they want to miss an occasion like that? Likewise, in an extreme way, some wise men followed a star to know where Jesus was born.

Both those groups of people would do all they could, even if that meant "having a little faith" to see and meet Jesus.

Our day of Christmas (in 2008) was an eventful day, from one thing to next, we were surrounded by people throughout the day, and as that day came to an end, I rested my head on my pillow and thought to myself, "what a day!"

Mary and Joseph (in AD 0), after a long day of many visits and being surrounded by farm animals were exhausted! After receiving gifts and hearing praise for their new-born son, Jesus – they rested their heads against the hay bundles and Mary thought: "What a day!"
*

What happened after that day when Jesus was born? Well, as the years went by Jesus had another birthday and another one after that and so on and so on - until at the right time - God's time: Jesus began His ministry. He started speaking and living out the truth and love that God Almighty (His heavenly Father) had sent him down to show and share. He started when He was 30. So, what was going on in those 30 years while Jesus was growing up? God was not resting - He was still reaching and preparing the hearts of Jesus and of the people...

Christmas 2008 has come and gone! The January Sales have come to an end, people work on losing their Christmas weight, adults go back to work and children back to school... and it seems as if Christmas didn't even happen. What is happening? Well, I can tell you what is not happening? God is not resting - He is still reaching and with the Holy Spirit and the gospel of Jesus (preached by ordinary people like you and I) – He is still preparing the hearts of the people...

Acknowledgements

Thanks to Rowena Gibbons, for proofreading the bigger stories. My use of *italics* and my silly grammar errors must have tested your patience. Thank you to Brad Coetzee (FAB Video Productions) for designing the front cover. Thanks to all my family, for encouraging me with my writing. Thanks to all my friends, who have spurred me on, and reminded me of my dream to get a physical book out there. Thanks to all those who have once said to me "You should write a book." Thanks too, for you who have purchased this book. (You are even reading, the acknowledgements?) I am grateful too, I guess, for a period of lockdown – which encouraged me to start writing again. Lastly, thank you to God for this gift of words He has given me. I love trying to see life through Your eyes.

Printed in Great Britain
by Amazon